A Snow Goose

& other utopian fictions

short stories by

JIM PERRIN

CinnamonPress

Published by Cinnamon Press, Meirion House, Tanygrisiau, Blaenau Ffestiniog, Gwynedd, LL41 3SU www.cinnamonpress.com

The right of Jim Perrin to be identified as author of this work has been asserted by him in accordance with the Copyright, Designs and Patent Act, 1988. © 2013 Jim Perrin.. ISBN 978-1-907090-92-9
British Library Cataloguing in Publication Data. A CIP record for this book can be obtained from the British Library.
Designed and typeset in Garamond by Cinnamon Press. Cover design by Jan Fortune
Cinnamon Press is represented by Inpress and by the Welsh Books Council in Wales.
Printed in Poland

The publisher acknowledges the support of the Welsh Books council

Acknowledgements

'A Snow Goose' first appeared in the anthology *Sea Stories* published by the National Maritime Museum, and is published here with their kind permission. 'The Eyas' was commissioned by James Robinson for the Radio Four series 'Modern Welsh Voices'. Particular thanks are due to the Welsh Books Council and Jan and Rowan Fortune at Cinnamon Press for suggesting and supporting this project. Heartfelt thanks, too, for sundry assistance, stimulation and friendship to Elizabeth Baker, Sally and Elis Baker-Jones, Mark Charlton, Mark Cocker, Melangell Dafydd, Iestyn Daniel, Hywel and Glenda Davies, Paul and Nancy Evans, Ian Gregson, Niall Griffiths and Deborah, Nicolette Hughes, Isobel MacLeod, Eric Morgan, Tony Shaw, Meic Stevens, Dicky Swinden, Amanda Townend and Jan Wolf.

Epigraph to the book W.B. Yeats, 'A Prayer for my daughter'

Epigraph to 'A Snow Goose' David C. Woodman, 'Inuit Accounts and the Franklin Mystery' is from *Echoing Silence: Essays on Arctic Narrative*, ed. John Moss, (University of Ottawa Press, 1997), p. 59. Used by kind permission.

Epigraph to 'After the Fall' from Rumi, 'Secret Places'.

Can'st thou pull out Leviathan with an sky-hook! is Herman Melville's paraphrasing of Job 41:1 in *Moby Dick*.

'Far, far below, and hazy with distance, he could see trees rising out of a narrow, shut-in valley.' and the paragraph beginning, *'...they fell a thousand feet,'* are from H. G. Wells' short story, 'The Country of the Blind'. Reprinted by permission of United Artists on behalf of: The Literary Executors of the Estate of H.G.Wells.

The paragraph beginning, *'A floodtide of screaming fiends and assassins and thieves and hirsute buggers pours forth into the universe...'* is from *Suttree* by Cormac McCarthy, (Picador, an imprint of Pan Macmillan), 2010, London. Used by kind permission.

'Miserere mei, Deus, omnis malignia discordia...' is from *Opera omnia in unum corpus digesta ad fidem editionum*

Coloniensium : cura et labore monachorum sacri ordinis Cartusiensis. Denis the Carthusian, 1402-1471.

'It may be, could we look with seeing eyes,' from 'Later Life: A Double Sonnet of Sonnets' by Christina Rossetti.

'Do not expect your heart to return...' from 'An Uplifting of the Heart', Rumi.

'Nothing in the world is single,...' from 'Love's Philosophy' by Percy Bysshe Shelley.

Epigraph to 'The Burning' from William James, *The Varieties of Religious Experience*.

'Fy newis I, rhiain firain feindeg,...' from *Llenyddiaeth y Cymry* by Hywel ab Owain Gwynedd.

'Mae'r blodau yn yr ardd yn hardd...' (The flowers aren't growing anymore) by Meic Stevens. Used by kind permission.

'The breath of her false mouth was like faint flowers,...' from 'Epipsychidion' by Percy Bysshe Shelley.

Quotation from T Gwynn Jones is from 'Ystrad Fflur' in *Caniadau* (Hughes a'i Fab, 1934) © Ystad ac eti feddion T Gwynn Jones cedwir pob hawl. Used by kind permission of Mrs Nonn Davies.

'...we were boyish dreamers in a world we did not know...' is from Idris Davies, 'An Untitled Poem'. Used by kind permission.

'Dewis gennyf i di; beth yw gennyd di fi?...' from Gogynfeirdd by Hywel ab Owen Gwynedd.

Epigraph to 'The Eyas' from *The Peregrine's Saga* by Henry Williamson © Henry Williamson Literary Estate. Used by kind permission.

'The low sun glowed the hawk's colours into rich relief:...' from J A Baker, *The Peregrine: The Hill of Summer & Diaries*. Reprinted by kind permission of HarperCollins Publishers Ltd © 2010.

By the same author:

Cwm Silyn & Cwellyn (with C.E.M. Yates)

Wintour's Leap

Mirrors in the Cliffs (ed.)

Menlove: The Life & Writings of John Menlove Edwards

On & Off the Rocks

A.A./O.S. Leisure Guide to Snowdonia

Yes, to Dance: Essays from Outside the Stockade

Visions of Snowdonia

Spirits of Place

River Map

Travels with The Flea & other Eccentric Journeys

The Villain: The Life of Don Whillans

The Climbing Essays

West: A Journey through the Landscapes of Loss

Snowdon: The Story of a Welsh Mountain

Shipton and Tilman: The Great Decade of Himalayan Exploration

Contents

Preface

After a long working life as a writer in thrall to the tyranny of facts, turning at last to imagined stories has been both revelation and delight. From earliest childhood I've read fiction avidly, and had never seriously considered writing it – until Cinnamon Press and the Welsh Books Council, in their wisdom and to whom my thanks, cornered me eighteen months ago with a commission to produce a collection on the strength of the one piece of imaginative writing I had published.

I was too busy at the time with a brace of volumes that needed careful and exact research. When they were done, tired and depleted I scanned around seeking models for the new book, the completion of which (and the delivery deadline!) suddenly felt daunting. I came quickly to a double conclusion.

Firstly, that there may be fashions but there are no inviolable rules in story-telling, whatever those adherents to the cult of 'creative writing' would have you believe; for rules are the means by which literary coteries erect their stockades, and the sacred duty of the writer, conversely, is to bear individual witness from outside any such defensive enclosure.

Secondly, that emulation – commonest of literary sins - is no way to proceed. I have my favourites, long and warmly admired; may 'sample' and allude at times in what follows; but I couldn't write like Katherine Mansfield or Ray Carver, Chekhov or Conrad, Coppard or Lawrence. And it seemed that to try to do so is to subvert what is always a writer's greatest gift, whatever the chosen genre: individuality of voice and perception.

Instead, I thought simply to try to say things that I had long wanted to say, but through a dialectic of the imagination rather than through one of factual presentation or polemic.

To do so involved the summoning of characters. Once you have made that supplication to the writing gods, what came as invigorating surprise was the autonomy of those you have called into being and accorded the freedom of the page. They lead you to places you did not think to go. They grow and change before your mind's eye. And they insist on their future lives too. I've not finished with any of the personalities who inhabit these tales, nor they with me I suspect. I hope you enjoy making their acquaintance as much as I have done, and that the short utopian narratives collected here will not be the last you hear of them.

Jim Perrin,
Ariege, May 2013

A Snow Goose

& other utopian fictions

For Hannah and Abi

If there's no hatred in a mind
Assault and battery of the wind
Can never tear the linnet from the leaf.

W.B. Yeats, 'A Prayer for my Daughter'

A Snow Goose

an historical eco-fable

By turning Franklin's men into bumbling Victorian caricatures who could not learn the lessons of survival, and by portraying the Inuit themselves as savage and ignorant people who did not know what was happening in their own land, we demean both parties.

David C. Woodman,
'Inuit Accounts and the Franklin Mystery'

June, 1848. As the main body of sailors hauling the boat on its sledge across the sea ice—smoother now than where their ships were beset a hundred miles round the coast to the north—disappeared behind the island in the strait, Solomon was the first to speak, voicing all their concerns:

'I wonder if we shall see those men again on this earth, Captain?'

'Better that they head south to the Fish River,' Crozier replied, a memory of his Irish upbringing in the throaty tones. 'If another winter is to be endured, Sergeant, the hunting there is what will see those men through. We all hunt for our lives now. As to the field hospital, Mr Peddle and Mr Stanley will do what they can to restore the men to health, and Commander FitzJames and Lieutenant Irving will get them back to the ships in due course.'

His words tailed off into a forlorn silence, as though unconvinced of their own meaning. With a shake of his head he gathered himself and picked up the train of thought again: 'The stores we left they might eke out for another year. If all goes well, the men at the river can return to provision them, and once we ourselves get free of this fearful place and send out word…'

Even as he spoke, he was weighing again the decision to split his surviving men into three groups. From being a newly enlisted boy sailing out of Cork on the *Hamadryad* thirty-eight years before, he had been used to his every action being dictated by custom, order and regulation. In the year since Sir John Franklin had died—with the crews on half-rations, and the paucity of those but little augmented by what they had been able to shoot or snare on the frozen northerly coast of King William Land or amidst the ridged and tortured ice close to the ships—ingrained habits had maintained not only the discipline, but even survival itself.

Now, all was open to question. It had been five weeks since *Erebus* and *Terror* were deserted. In that time they had covered barely three miles a day, and nine more men had died. To separate was imperative if any were to live. His second in command, FitzJames, of whose mental fortitude Crozier harboured grave doubts, was too weak physically to travel much further. Despite which, he had to take overall charge at the hospital tents in Terror Bay. Crozier knew it to be a bad option, but it was the one that regulation and necessity decreed. Three of the five remaining lieutenants were among those who had succumbed to scurvy or pneumonia on the march south. Of the two still living, Irving would stay with FitzJames and Hodgson was leading the men across the ice. Splitting the party, Crozier had reasoned, and sending the strongest ahead in two groups— the larger one to establish a camp on the mainland to hunt, his own to find some way through the Arctic maze—was surely the last and only chance. If he and the six men here under his command were to survive, he knew that another model of conduct was needed, at odds with all his training. They must move light and fast through this alien land. Continually this last year, flickering through his mind had come images of the Eskimo community at Igloolik, and the winter he had spent there with Parry twenty-five years before.

Ignorant and uncultivated savages, unspeakable in their personal habits and morality, his fellow officers would always opine; though those same officers, the Irishman noted, were not above availing themselves of these 'savages' favours, be they men or women. But in Crozier, himself at a distance from established attitudes through his Irish accent and long ascent through the ranks, the memory of Eskimo friendship and resourcefulness, the recognition of what was entailed in their long survival here, was growing daily now into admiration, curiosity, respect. He remembered his excursions from Igloolik with the hunters, strove to recall the Inuk word old Aua had taught him. *Quinuituq*—that was it—deep patience! The patience of a hunter, harpoon at the ready, waiting by an *aglu*—the breathing hole of a seal; the stillness of a man as he draws his bowstring and watches the inquisitive approach of a caribou. *Quinuituq*—he mouthed the word to himself again. If there were a key to his men's survival here, surely the Eskimos and not the traditions of the Royal Navy were its custodians?

As their captain sat in silent thought, as if to dissipate the pensive mood descending upon them, his men set to loading their scant equipment, supplies and the gutta-percha Halkett boat onto the lightened sledge. Close by, a wheatear bobbed and scurried over frozen gravel. Blankey, the *Terror*'s ice-master, watched its progress, catching his captain's eye and exchanging glances.

'Come, Sergeant,' the captain spoke, 'and you, Mr Blankey, let us spy out the lie of the land.'

The marine picked up his musket, the ice-master a fowling-piece, and they followed Crozier as he climbed the brief slope. At its crest, Crozier crouched and gestured the two men urgently down. They crawled on to join him, small stones trickling into the heels of their sea boots through split and abraded seams. In front of them as they peered over, drumlins ranged north-west and south-east like shorn sheep flocking away over the mottled plain. There, a hundred paces beneath them, a first migratory caribou nuzzled at the snow, unaware of their presence.

'Watch now, Sergeant,' he whispered, 'and I guarantee it will come within twenty paces—aim for the heart.'

Slowly Crozier raised himself to his knees, head bowed and arms held high above as though he were an antlered beast. The caribou ceased browsing under the snow and turned quizzically to watch. It moved towards the men's hiding place, stopping here and there to nose at the ground, then lifting its head again and fastening a myopic gaze upon the sentinel at the hilltop. Hammer of his musket cocked, Tozer sighted down the long barrel. He remembered the contorted face of the first man he had killed—the soldier of Mehemet Ali's at Acre eight years before—remembered that then too life and death were in the balance; not slowly, as here, with disease and starvation its agents, but hovering on the point of a spear.

Barely resolving themselves into thought, his instincts turned from heat-of-the-moment action back to this watchful, silent intensity. The caribou ambled a few more paces towards them, sniffing at the air. The three men held their frozen tableau. The caribou trotted closer, halted, lifted a rear leg and turned to rub muzzle against flank as Tozer eased back the trigger, stock firm against his shoulder as the hammer struck. Powder fizzed, and the spinning ball grazed past bone to burst the animal's heart. Feet flailing, it rolled, twitched and was still, echo of the shot rolling out across the island.

'Well done, Sergeant—call the men and haul it down. We'll gralloch the beast, eat and then press on.'

Soon the caribou's belly was slit and its viscera spread out by the sledge.

'The stove, sir…' asked the sergeant. In reply, Crozier took his knife and hacked the steaming liver into seven chunks. When he'd finished he raised one to his mouth and bit off a piece, gesturing the men to follow suit. Hesitant, almost aghast, torn briefly between hunger and habit, they each picked up their portion and fell to.

'On all my voyages, I never saw an Eskimo with the scurvy. And yet we sailors always suffer. Think on that… I'm sorry, gentlemen, that we have no dinner service, nor lemon juice left to dress your meat. But nor did I ever meet the Eskimo who had use for those items, and it seems to me that we must now copy their ways. I oftentimes saw them stuff their mouths with blubber straight from white whale or seal, have tried it myself on occasion and suspect it has qualities of which we stand here sorely in need. Hot liver and raw heart for our luncheon then, friends, rare steak when we sup tonight, and we shall live to see England's shores again. A little fortitude in the matter of diet now, and Greenhithe will soon enough see you carousing along Grope Alley once more.'

And so the men dined—the marine sergeant Tozer; the whaling-fleet ice-master Blankey; seaman Manson from Whitby, who had often been north with the latter; *Terror*'s captain of the maintop Tom Farr, its coxswain John Wilson, and Osmer, the paymaster from *Erebus*. Apart from Osmer, who had been urged upon him, these were the few men still living whom he had come to trust and respect from among the assembly of Arctic tyros and those favourites of the Admiralty favourite FitzJames who had so dismayed Crozier before the expedition set sail three years ago. In Crozier's view they were smooth young gentlemen adventurers; untested in battle, without instinct for this elemental place where his own rough and hard-won knowledge surely demanded precedence—and would now take it. His responsibility as captain apart, every step away from FitzJames and the continual reproach of his polished manners and brilliant conversation assuaged bitter pangs of resentment.

Wiping the blood from cracked and blackened lips and greying beards with handfuls of snow or tattered cuffs, they loaded the carcase onto the sledge, and with a new vigour bent to the traces and hauled it back onto the ice. Behind them, a flash of white beneath the wings and the high, pealing cry of a skua caused Blankey to glance over his shoulder to where the dark bird had swooped and snatched a length of the caribou's discarded guts, trailing it across the snow. With an involuntary shudder, his cleated boot soles slipping briefly, he fell back into step.

With their captain out in front, they turned to the north-east and set a steady rhythm. The ice here in the great bay that stretched across to the mouth of the Fish River, away from the jostling and shrieking stream of pack that surged down from the Beaufort Sea, was glassy and smooth. Here and there they splashed through puddles that told of encroaching spring, or skirted round melt-holes from which, at a distance, seals watched. The sledge slid easily and the labour was light compared with hauling the boats down from Victory Point over the pressure ridges and the fractured leads. Tom Farr sang to himself as they pulled:

'*The sea, the sea, the open sea, it grew so fresh the ever-free…*'

'What's that you're groaning out, Tom?' asked Sol Tozer.

'Why, 'tis a little lament in the key of C for the delights of a life upon the land that my captain of the foretop, Mr Peglar, and I would often sing—the slip of that warm liver down my throat has put me much in mind of it.'

Before the sergeant could voice his ribald reply, Captain Crozier gestured shorewards to a shingle beach at the back of a rocky cove, sheltered from the winds.

'We shall camp there and eat well tonight, men. Come…'

The ice of the cove gleamed in morning sunlight as Tom Farr pissed against a rock wall. He looked at the dribble of thick yellow and viscous liquid that stained a shadowed drift of snow with distaste, fastened his breeches and walked down the shingle, his six companions still sleeping behind him. He gazed over the ice, studying its fractured patterns and monotone textures—gauzy, clear, opalescent—and wondered how so beautiful a substance could be so cruel, unpredictable, entrapping. How often had the same dilemma exercised him through the long months of imprisonment in the northern pack? He remembered climbing time after time to the crow's-nest to scan the horizon, always seeing the same infinite variety within monotony and emptiness. A rock round the corner of the cove shone strangely. He walked on to look at it, losing sight of the camp. Further still, he knelt by another rock to examine the contained and exquisite vigour, the brilliant colours of the lichens that had caught his attention, their names unknown to him: jewel lichen, map lichen, sunburst lichen. In a moment of vision, their seamed and flaky growths, slow-colonising, rustling out from dead and hollow centres in ages of infinite patience, were to him the true Arctic hearts. As he was absorbed, lost and insentient to all but the focus of his thought and eyes, where these and the forms of beauty he had known, whether of ocean skies or the green life of land or the secret and exotic petalled flesh between a woman's thighs, seemed entirely as one—in that moment of reverie, without uttering a cry, he was dead, his neck broken by a single blow of the stalking bear's paw as it pounced. Before his companions were awake to his absence, he was torn and chewed meat digesting in the belly of the beast as it padded silently away, back into the frozen land.

Manson, who had survived the press of 1835 in Baffin Bay, made the discovery. He saw at once what had happened, and that Farr was beyond help. Blood was spattered across the snow-patched beach where the bear had hurled his lifeless body around like a terrier with a child's toy. The seaman hastened back across the shingle to rouse and inform his captain. All six men gathered, silently building a cairn of splintered rocks over their companion's remains. When they had finished, they stood bareheaded in a cold, crystal wind as Crozier stumbled through words by now known almost by heart. At the camp they lit the spirit stove, thawed and breakfasted with scant appetite on what remained in the iron kettle of last night's feast. Would they track and kill the bear? asked Manson's old shipmate from the *Viewforth*, Blankey. But he, the captain, all of them, knew that their strength was too fragile for that, and their supplies too scant. They would press on eastwards, hoping for better hunting grounds beyond the land-bridge they believed led across to Boothia, Fury Bay, Igloolik and perhaps even home. Henceforth, muskets would be loaded and no man would venture alone out of sight. They rattled the sledge out onto the ice once more, and headed into the sun.

After four hours of hauling along a coast that ran northerly now, the men's breeches and boots soaked with splashing through meltwater shallows, they pulled out on to a rackety stone beach down which ran a freshet of good water from the thawing ground behind. As the men filled the stove and set the great black kettle to boil, Crozier took out his telescope and scanned across the bight. Fixing on a point at the back of the bay, excitedly he called the ice-master Blankey and Osmer across, handing Osmer the telescope as he arrived.

'I was told, sir, by men that have spoken with them of something the Eskimos of Baffin Bay believe. Far to the west of Igloolik and the lands of its people, they say there lives a tribe called the Netsilik. The people at Igloolik, it's said, hunt walrus, but the Netsilik are expert at catching seal —a more difficult, albeit less dangerous task.'

'Indeed, Mr Osmer, I heard a great deal about them in my time at Igloolik. It is a great mistake to assume likeness among all those we choose to term 'savages'. My friends of Igloolik, for example, were a good-natured and playful people, uxorious and happy. But I heard from them that those of Netsilik were quarrelsome, warlike and conversant with all the forms of Eskimo magic. They live in a place known as Uqsuqtuuq, which I was told translated as the place where plenty of blubber was to be had. From the look of the encampment yonder, I would say, Mr Osmer, that the soubriquet is apt.'

'That sounds like the language of Commander FitzJames,' responded the former paymaster of the *Erebus*, to Crozier's obvious displeasure, 'but if I understand your meaning aright, then this encampment surely is Uqsuqtuuk, and if their reputation is deserved, we do well to keep our weapons primed. Perhaps by means of that magic we shall ensure their cooperation?'

'I think, Mr Osmer, that a watchful diplomacy will be our first line of defence. Another haunch of caribou tonight, and tomorrow we shall introduce ourselves, I fancy. Our presence, of course, will already have been observed.'

The men hauled the sledge up to a sheltered recess in the rocks, propped loaded guns against it and made camp. Manson, with studied delicacy, peeled back hide, removed a leg from the caribou carcase and carved chunks of it into the kettle to boil whilst the others stamped cold feet and smoked short pipes. It was Osmer, standing apart from the other men and reflecting on the captain's quick rebuff, who saw the bear first. It was ambling along the ice, and it was coming in their direction. 'Sir!' he called, and gestured towards it.

Crozier assessed the situation and calmly gave out orders: 'Sergeant Tozer—move forty paces down the beach to the right. A shot from the side for its heart. Manson, on the left thirty paces; wait until it's broadside to you. Mr Osmer, Mr Blankey—behind the sledge with the fowling-pieces, and you and I, Mr Wilson, must rely on sword and pistol to give the men time to reload if it comes to that.'

The bear, as he was speaking, shambled on purposefully towards the scent of cooking meat, its low head moving from side to side, breast still faintly red from its morning feast.

'So, Mr Blankey, your friend will have his revenge,' the captain murmured, the soft shift of shingle under the bear's weight whispering as it approached. It hesitated, sensing men to the left and right, and began to lope forward. Unerringly, the marine sharpshooter's ball crashed through its ribs to the heart, and as it flailed and reared Manson's bullet pierced the belly and shattered its spine. Suddenly Blankey was vaulting the sledge and running to where the animal writhed. From ten feet he stood and delivered both barrels of heavy shot, punching through its ribs into its heart. With a last surge of strength it lunged for the ice-master, pinning him to the ground as the captain's sword sliced through its throat and Wilson's pistol discharged through its eye into the brain. A great tremor shook the vast body, coughing gouts of blood across Blankey, and with a final faint convulsion the creature died. Wrenching out his sword, the captain wiped it across the dingy yellow pelt as Tozer and Manson ran across, muskets reloaded.

'Mr Blankey…' called the captain to the crushed and blood-sodden figure under the bear.

'Aye, Captain,' came the response. 'All's well, but 'tis a heavy kind of blanket I'm lying under. I'd be grateful if you'd get me out from under here.'

Sobs of laughter greeted his words. The men took position to heave away the animal's corpse. As they did so, with unanimous instinct they glanced over at the sledge, from behind which peered the pale face of Charles Osmer.

Orpingalik arrived that night. He pushed back the pointed hood of his caribou-skin coat and called the white men, whose language he spoke, *qallunaat*. He himself, he told them, was an *angakoq*—a shaman, as they eventually came to understand. All of them would later swear that as he walked unexpectedly up the beach in midnight twilight, making them reach for the guns, he was surrounded with a shimmering and fiery light which caused the superstitious among them to believe they were encountering a ghost. But he ate the remnants of their evening meat with corporeal relish, and later withdrew a small distance to converse with Crozier, whom he addressed as Aglooka. He told of how, days earlier, hunters of his tribe had met with the other Aglooka, the weak boy in the blue coat with gold at the shoulders, who had begged seal-meat of them for himself and his three companions. He was going to die soon, Orpingalik stated, and that was his fate.

'But you, Aglooka the man, known by our people to the east, who has brought Nanuq as gift to our tribe and can hunt for yourself in this land—you will stay with us through winters to come and father children of our tribe. Though you will not see them grow into men, for like the snow geese, you will fly south before your bones whiten here. Now I will dance for you and your men, Aglooka.'

Orpingalik stepped down to a flat stretch of shingle, stilled himself and started to dance. At first he was slow, the movement studied, cautious, stealthy, deliberate, but building into a sinuous, sure, rhythmical, intertwining ecstasy, stooping, coiling, circling, pirouetting low above the beach, his expression rapt, hypnotically intense, hands always describing, floating, shaping pictures for his watchers' imaginations to grasp; of his prey, conjured up for them, immanent, there. Later the white men would talk of the presences they had seen. All around Orpingalik as he danced, the shimmering light, as though he had stepped straight from the waves, dripping phosphorescence. And as he danced, he sang this song:

> I remember Nanuq, the white one,
> The great white bear.
> With back and haunches high
> And snout in the snow he walked,
> He alone in the belief of his maleness.
>> He ran towards me.
>> *Unaya, Unaya!*

> Down I was thrown, again, again,
> Until, breathless, he lay to rest,
> Ignorant that I was his fate,
> Through whom his end would come,
> Fooled in thinking he only was male.
>> I too was a man!
>> *Unaya, Unaya!*

When Orpingalik had finished, he turned to Crozier: 'Aglooka, tomorrow you come with your hunters to Uqsuqtuuq. Bring your gift on the sledge for my people to see, and we will welcome you there.' With that, he walked down the beach and on to the ice, where his mercury shimmering was absorbed into the shadowy, pewter dim.

As they approached the village, dogs along the beach left off gnawing the bones of caribou and bellowed their protest. Men, women and children ran down onto the ice, calling out to Nanuq where he lay, jaws agape and snarling atop the sledge. They crowded onto the traces and heaved the load up into the village, where women using the *ulu* were scraping fat from the skins of Arctic foxes stretched on frames. A smell of boiling seal meat hung round the low stone houses. Where the ice on the sunlit side of the bay had melted, scalloped and glistening little icebergs with turquoise melt-pools on their tops floated in the sea. The women unloaded the bear and the caribou carcase and immediately started dismembering them, teasing out sinews from flesh, scraping fat from hoof and paw into bags of salmon skin, butchering the meat into ever-smaller joints, discarding only the liver of Nanuq. The six white men were ushered into the *qaggeg*—the largest dwelling in the village, where the smell of burning seal fat from the *kudlik* was overpowering and a flickering light from its moss wicks cast strange and moving shadows. Orpingalik was waiting for them there, seated on a stone bench covered with the winter hide of caribou. He gestured Crozier to walk with him to the door of the hut.

'See there, Aglooka, that far hill?'

He pointed west to where an ice mirage, a long, low chimera of a sky-hill, glimmered along the horizon.

'That is Uvayok. Before death arrived on earth a race of immortal giants lived in the north of Qiiliniq. But one summer there was no food, the walrus and the bowhead whale had disappeared, so the giants set off towards the south. South took them further from food, and so they starved. Uvayok was the largest of them. In time his body sank into the soil and the small flowers of summer grew over him until only a rib showed here and there and he became a hill. Lakes formed from the liquid that drained from his bladder. Fish swam in those lakes, and the loons called from them. Aglooka, these are our stories, the stories of the land to which you must listen now. You, and the *qallunaat* with arrow feathers on his coat…'

Orpingalik glanced and nodded to the marine sergeant.

'…you will stay here with us, hunt seal and the white whales and geese. Those other men will cross the ice before it breaks up, and will live at Taloyoak. They will kill caribou. This way, all will eat. We have lost many hunters in two springs. My daughter's husband was one of them. The women become dangerous when they have no husbands to lie with them. You white men who are strong and can hunt will take their place.'

That night, as they feasted in the *qaggeg* on seal meat, and caribou, and fermented walrus intestine that tasted within the skin like strong cheese, Crozier reflected how easily responsibility gave way to compliance in the face of greater knowledge. His fate was to have arrived here. That of those others who might still survive was now in their own hands, and he was absolved of it. After all had eaten, the women removed the blackened kettles from the *kudlik*, trimmed the wicks and recharged the trough with seal fat. Story-songs and dancing entertained them, and between the *qallunaat* and the young and widowed women glances flickered. Crozier remembered his proposal to Franklin's niece Sophie, the disdain with which it was received, the averted eyes and the sidelong quick glances as she talked later with her Aunt Jane, the scalding tinkle of their laughter. He caught a young woman's eye and thought how different was the frank and unabashed interest of her gaze. Observing them, Orpingalik whispered to him: 'Aglooka, this is Uvlunuaq, my daughter.'

Later that night, she led him back to her house, where, by the light of the *kudlik*, she took the long sticks called *tuglirak* from her hair so that it fell over her shoulders, and slipped out of her fur clothing to stand naked in front of him. Laughing, she unfastened the buttons of his frayed uniform, pulled down his breeches, helped him out of stained and ragged linen. His arms encircled her as she stood close, her breasts against his chest, feeling him rise against her. With a cracked hand, he sought out and caressed the velvet moist of her, her salt savour stinging in the split tips of his fingers: 'A man must be patient to give a woman pleasure,' she pouted, squirming away, pushing him down merrily onto the sleeping platform and tumbling with him between the heavy winter hides of caribou.

A decade passed as quickly as the bloom of fireweed in a summer season. Aglooka and the *qallunaat*-with-arrows-on-his-coat lived with their wives in Uqsuqtuuq, knowing from the other hunters that the ships had drifted away and sunk and their erstwhile companions along the northern coast were all dead. But they shunned those places where their uncovered bones lay. Children were born, as Orpingalik had promised, and when the attending women called him in to hold the squalling bundle, black-haired and red of face, Aglooka was amazed by the overpowering rush of love he felt for each one of them. Between him and Uvlunuaq too the warm laughter, the cooperation and the mutual learning flowered into understanding and a slow fondness of passion.

News came from Taloyoak, to the north across the long strait: of Wilson's uncanny expertise with a dog team ('What's a coxswain but the handler of a bunch of old sea dogs?' chuckled Aglooka, remembering a former life); of his and Blankey's journey to Fury Beach, from the cache of stores at which they had brought back muskets, and a great quantity of black powder and shot, some of which made its way back to Uqsuqtuuq in the *umiak*—the women's boat— in the summer Uvlunuaq's first-born had died.

One spring Wilson and his dogs sledged over the ice, and filled out detail for Aglooka of the rumours he had heard about Osmer's death: he had forced the wife of Ugarng whilst the latter was hunting. Before the men came back, the women had overpowered him. They had stripped him, tethered him spreadeagled to stakes of sharpened caribou bone, had cut off his genitals, put them in his mouth and left him on the slope above the summer camp in the hills for predators. The parasitic jaegers had taken out his eyes. Nanuq and his attendant daemon, the little Arctic fox, had feasted on what was left. Manson had been killed by a charging musk ox. Blankey had a wife and many children.

One year a strange *qallunaat* had come by land from the south with dogs, and the village had sold him useless things from the ships, but told him nothing of the two *qallunaat* married to women of the village who had just left for the summer camp to hunt caribou, or of those across the water.

He went away, but Aglooka knew he and his kind would be back, and Uvlunuaq knew too, as they and their children held close under the heavy hides in the dark of winter. She knew that the autumn of his life was settling on her man. In their tenth spring together, she sewed new boots for him, lined with the fur of *Nanuq*, soled with the skin of bearded seal and stitched with caribou sinews, which swelled when wet to make them waterproof.

She fashioned his coat of sealskin because she knew he would be going south, and on the morning when she heard the skeins flying high over the bay she slipped from the bed, stood so that he might see her naked for the last time and sang him this song:

> I will walk with leg muscles
> Strong as shin-sinew of the caribou calf.
> I will walk with leg muscles
> Strong as shin-sinew of the white hare.
> Carefully I will turn from the dark.
> I will head into the light of day.

She dressed him, tied packages of seal meat on his sledge, drums of powder and shot, a snow knife and a heavy sleeping hide. Months later, by Angikuni Lake on the Kazan River in Keewatin, Aglooka lifted the heavy fowling-piece to the hole in the canvas screen as the snow geese, black primaries stark against their brilliant white, wheeled in to land in the shallows.

The largest of them began to walk towards his hiding place over stony slopes, ground thawed billowy and summer-soft, the surface litter of stone graded into parallel or polygonal abstractions. A pair of snow buntings scurried past.

The goose paused to graze the minimal low plants that crouched beneath a dry, harsh wind—saxifrages and sedums, the roseroot and mountain avens, the cinquefoils and grass of Parnassus and fragrant shield fern, bog cotton ever-moving, the polar willow, slender-shooted, its leaves a muted, dark and unassertive green. It scratched its long neck against an old bone from the caribou herds, honeycombed and grey, mottled, with the appearance of bleached and seasoned timber, the mosses growing over it. As it did so, Aglooka's finger tensed on the trigger and squeezed.

The flash as the worn and rusting barrel split seared his eyes, a splinter of pitted steel bedded in his throat. He wrenched it free, and in doing so the razor edge cut the artery and his blood pumped out in a dying rhythm. The high tumbling calls of the geese as they hurled away across the sky, heading south, registered faintly in his fading consciousness.

His last breath rattled out in a red froth. Coyote and wolf spread his bones, the snows of winter shrouding them, and those of all the lost who would never be found.

After the Fall

a utopian fantasy

Lovers find secret places
inside this violent world
where they make transactions
with beauty.

Rumi, 'Secret Places'

His picks thudded into the snow-ice. Moss hauled himself out on to the broad shelf, stamped his crampons to gain a good footing, and peered back down the glistening ice-runnel to where Rigby crouched under a bulging rock one hundred and forty feet below.

'I'm there,' he yelled, wind carrying his words away but his meaning made plain as he tugged at the twin ropes that connected them. He drew a great hank through a sparse and rattling punctuation of karabiners and ice-screws, and took a last long look down the ridge they had climbed. Their first attempt on it had taken eighteen days in all—ferrying the supplies their four Sherpas had brought up through the ice-fall and hanging glacier to a dump in the big bergschrund; gaining the rock and moving up scoured slabs to gain the dragon's crest; hauling heavy sacs of equipment, fuel and provisions to the notch behind the huge satellite pinnacle from where their route started in earnest. Then came the intense labour, the excruciating technicalities of the initial twelve thousand-foot vertical wall above the notch. Up that smooth and compact rock they had followed the thinnest of incipient seams, progress achingly slow as they slipped skyhooks on to tiny edges or hammered copperheads and bashees against the crystals and vague indentations, annealing soft metal on to rough rock-surfaces until body-weight could tenuously be held.

Each method allowed Moss—the older and lighter, more competent and experienced of the two men—to clip in a karabiner, attach a tape stirrup and teeter up until at full stretch another slight depression or cluster of crystals offered itself up to malleable copper and precise hammer-blows. Acclimatized as he was, at an altitude already above twenty-thousand feet his breathing at each effort was laboured, stertorous. He was painfully aware that should one point of attachment fail the whole sequence would unzip and he'd be flailing through the air down to where Rigby stamped the circulation into his feet—and then an equal distance beyond before the rope could arrest his descent, if Rigby had his wits about him and his belay held.

Every fifty feet, if he found a suitable pocket or vague crack, Moss took out the star-drill, hammering and twisting precariously until he'd made a shallow hole into which he could tap a metal sleeve and hammer home the expansion bolt that ensured a greater modicum of security. With a hundred and sixty feet of rope out, he arrived at a ledge eight inches wide. At last he could stand in balance. After excruciating labour he placed two good bolts. He clipped into them, secured himself, took in the slack rope between himself and Rigby and then clipped the static line he'd been talked into trailing to one of the bolts.

'OK Joe,' he yelled down. 'You can jumar now.'

Rigby fitted the jumars on to the arcing rope, his weight gradually taking up the stretch, reining in the catenary as he moved each toothed clamp upwards. He juddered up to his leader, stripping the aid with jerks and flailing hammer blows and clipping it to his bandolier as he climbed. Moss watched his second's spasmodic progress critically, replaying in his mind the boastful assurances of competence, the hard-man posturings, the claimed ascents about which, from anomalous and contradictory details, increasingly he had come to harbour doubts. At least, he reassured himself, Rigby had been up for it—had protested enthusiasm and ability for their two-man attempt even when faced with the scariest set of mountain photographs Moss himself had ever seen.

'Parasco Shar! It's the last Leviathan!' he'd told Rigby, 'the only remaining twenty-five thousander still unclimbed —and looking at these you can quite see why.'

'Brilliant!' Rigby had said. 'When are we going? We'll make a million. And I'll pinch that title for my book. *The Last Leviathan*! Sounds great, doesn't it! *Can'st thou pull out Leviathan with an sky-hook*! Know where that's from?'

'*Book of Job*,' thought Moss, remembering back to schooldays at Xaverian, and the notion that he had a vocation for the priesthood, 'I'm beginning to recognize most of your sources.'

What he spoke aloud was this: 'So you're to be writer-in-residence, are you? What about a million each? When you get to fall off, I could do what Whymper was accused of having done on the Matterhorn, and cut the rope. That'd make a true-life adventure of it.'

Behind the sardonic response, Moss never doubted which of them would likely be taking a fall. But Rigby was lost in a reverie, already counting out the cash, milking the acclaim.

By the time the rumours had begun to reach Moss— doubts, aspersions, mocking comments about the Munchausen dimension to the string of adventure stories Rigby had published in *Out There* magazine—flights had been booked, sponsorship and grants were in place.

'Watch it with that one, mate—he's a one-man disaster area! A catastrophe on every trip—or so he says…'

Too late for reflection on his own judgement now. Moss was committed to what, if successful, would be one of the most ambitious alpine-style ascents in mountaineering history. And he knew from the first day's approach up the glacier that his companion was not the climber he claimed to be.

'My own stupid fault,' he berated himself, taking in the slack as Rigby hacked his way up the fixed rope. 'If I'd just bitten my tongue a few times, held back from holding up the mirror to bullshit and vanity, maybe I could have been here with someone better able to take his share of the climbing.'

'Or her share,' he reminded himself ruefully, wincing at memory of Lynette's words as they'd split last year. 'Monomanic. Obsessive. Brutally judgmental. You're just a climbing machine, not a human being. You're not good boyfriend material. I don't love you any more. I'm not going on any more of your ego-trips… Better things to do with my life… You can't even be bothered with making love to me any more.'

In self-reassurance, he asked himself how else you could be expected to stay alive in these harshest of the world's environments except by adopting the most hard-faced and critical awareness, preparing yourself for every risk. But he also remembered the feel and musky scent of her in those charged morning moments in hotel-room or tent or in their Sheffield flat when he'd slipped out of bed and away from her as she'd opened herself to him, sleepily, sensually; when he'd insisted on forcing them out into the harsh dimensions of the crags day after day, or up into the knifing winds and on to the ice-rimed rocks of Scottish winter mountains in his quest for a perfectly-honed expertise, for ever-higher numbers by which their achievements were graded and his prowess as leader defined.

'Early communion again, is it?' had been her increasingly acerbic refrain, before she'd started to find excuses not to go: work, friends' parties, the spare ticket for Glyndebourne her parents down in Worthing had bought.

Yet now, isolated and miserable after their split, proscribed within the mountaineering community for his stringent attitudes despite the successes and survival they'd enabled, he'd let his guard lapse. He'd drifted into the situation of being on the most audacious ascent of his climbing career with a companion who seemed barely technically competent. He was certainly far less so than Lynette. And there was a deeper irritant. With every day he and Rigby kept company, and with every evening's conversation they shared, new stories laced with oddity, contradiction, borrowed echo, lack of confirming witnesses, were put forward. Rigby appeared to him more and more as a dubious and bullshitting buffoon, and in his daily demeanour an obstreperous bully to go with it, vile towards the Sherpas, ill-tempered, selfish, arrogant. And if ever an environment was calculated to breed and intensify dislike, it's that of the mountaineering expedition—marriage is a breeze by comparison.

'There's karma for you!' he said out loud, reflecting on the justice of those accusations from Lynette. Swallowing the rising flood of animus towards Rigby, he took the rope in snug to the latter's harness to stop him swinging across beneath a line of massive overhangs, and shouted down a few words of encouragement, desiring the ascent more than the sour gratification of truth-telling. Rigby floundered up panting alongside him at the tiny ledge, steadied himself, and was tied in. Moss transferred the gear from his bandolier, clipped the trail-rope back into his harness, pushed the lead-ropes into Rigby's belay-plate, and set off again.

So it went on, that day and the next. They fixed lengths of static line between good anchor-points on the most awkward stretches, and as night fell descended rapidly down these to spend a comfortable night in the notch, where food and fuel was plentiful. At least Rigby was careful and competent about the descent. Morning found them jumaring back to their high point. The wall gave nine pitches of the most difficult aid-climbing Moss had ever done. He was entirely absorbed in the task, blinkered almost, barely aware even of his companion. The savage beauty of the mountain around him was entirely occluded by his concentration on a few square feet of grained surface in front of his face. Just occasionally, sensed at the margins of vision, it would register momentarily on his consciousness, and as quickly put aside. Beauty was a dangerous distraction to the Calvinist he felt every top climber must be. Small wonder his Catholicism and all its sense of ritual had been put in reserve.

The effort of two days brought them finally to where the great vertical rock-gable of the ridge eased over into a narrow crest soaring up, he estimated, for another two thousand feet to the apparent summit—though the ambiguous evidence of those terrifying telephoto shots taken by the Poles from Amarkanta Parbat had suggested this was an illusion. A broad snow-ramp, invisible from below, slipped across on to the right flank, and from it a shallow runnel, a trap-dyke filled with hard ice—one of those geological gifts that are the climber's delight—rose in a continuous white depression to the apex. At the head of the ramp there was even a kind of cave that, with a little hacking and clearing of pendent ice and chopping and smoothing of snow, gave them a comfortable bivouac site, sheltered and spacious. By the time they'd finished their preparation, it was mid-afternoon.

'We'll head back down the ropes to the notch for tonight, Joe. Tomorrow we'll do a couple of trips to stock the cave, bring up more fixed line, and then press on for the top of the ridge and the traverse.'

'The traverse?'

'Yeah. That's not the top we can see up there, I'm sure of that. What worries me is what the ridge between it and the real summit's going to be like. That's why we need to provision this camp, in case we have to beat a retreat and wait for the weather.'

'Weather looks good to me…'

'Never rely on it,' Moss replied, and under his breath he mouthed, 'Never rely on anything but yourself.'

Three days later, after exhausting labour the cave was stocked with reserves of food, fuel, long reels of static line. And the weather had held. Equipment for ice-climbing now replaced that for rock. As the blackness of night greying towards dawn, Moss set a billy of snow on the stove to melt and gave Rigby's recumbent form a prod with his toe. A few muttered obscenities hissed from within the sleeping bag. Moss packed more snow into the billy and contemplated hands mangled against lancet-crystalline rock. Ten minutes later he threw a teabag into the tepid, murky liquid, added sugar and milk powder, shared out the brew into two plastic mugs and handed one across, cramming yet more snow into the billy and setting it back on the stove as he did so.

'Stir yourself now…'

Rigby struggled into a sitting position, reached a hand out of his sleeping bag for the brew. An hour later they were ready, rucksacks packed. Moss uncoiled the ropes and tied on. Soon he was progressing methodically up the runnel, picks and front-points beating out a steady, slow, fracturing rhythm against his breathing's laboured insistency.

Two more days of labour, ice-screws and static line fixed over the whole length of the runnel, and Moss pulled himself free from gravity's demands to stand on the broad shelf of the false summit. He placed a camming device and a rock-piton in a shattered outcrop and brought up Rigby. Together they looked along a fretted thin crest of ice and snow that stretched for half-a-mile to the true summit. Beneath it the face dropped eight thousand feet to the glacier, lower down, and beside its moraine was the base camp they had last left five days before.

'Shit!' gasped Rigby. 'I'm not going along that! Are you crazy or what…'

'Any better ideas, then?'

'How about going down? We've made the summit.'

'Take another look, buddy—that's the summit, over there…'

'We'll call this the south summit. Who's to know it's not highest?'

'The whole world, eventually, and that's not the point. We'll dig in here for the night and see how things go tomorrow.'

'What about going back down to the cave?'

'Too much effort and time. We've got all we need up here. We can go rub our noses against it in the morning, see what it's really like.'

'What about that face?'

'What about it?'

'Has it ever been tried?'

'I thought you were the great student of mountaineering history. See that rib running up to half-height left of centre…'

Rigby nodded, peering.

'That's the line of the Nunez-Pointer attempt—pretty visionary for forty years ago.'

'What happened?'

'Nunez was one of that crazy Basque generation who were doing everything at the time. Wilson interviewed him for *Mountain* magazine. He said it was either climbing or ETA when he was a kid, those were the choices, and he didn't fancy dying in a Spanish gaol. You see the flat-iron at the top of the rib? Well he and Pointer, who was quite good for his time, mate of Bonington's, a pretty stolid Brit from the Anglo-Spanish expedition that's the only other one apart from us to try the peak, made it that far and Pointer, as far as you can make out from his account—he died in that big tragedy on Distaghil Sar a couple of years later—was pretty freaked, insisted they go down. So Nunez just headed off by himself—must have taken the rising diagonal you can see starting from just above the flat-iron that comes out on the ridge just below the summit. I think it's another trap-dyke—very useful. They'd fixed ropes as far as they got, Pointer scuttled off down them, and it's generally assumed Nunez made the top and died on the descent.'

'If it's already been done, we don't need to do it, then.'

'Stow it, and let's get organized.'

They chopped and kicked out a platform in the snow, hung a bivouac tent attached to the belays across it, and climbed in.

'That ridge looks suicidal to me,' Rigby whined once they were safely inside, but there was no answer. Moss was organizing food and drink. Eventually he looked across at Rigby.

'I suppose this must remind you of that story you tell about being in a bivouac at the top of the Walker, the ledge you were on collapsing and the pair of you left hanging off one creaking peg and having to be helicoptered off—who were you with that day, incidentally? I've always wondered.'

'No-one you'd know.'

'Funny that—I do know a guy to whom something very similar happened, and in exactly the same place. Feargal Davison—you know him, don't you?'

'Not that I recall.'

'He says you worked together at Mountain Mirage in Fort Bill that summer—seems to think you borrowed his story for some article you wrote.'

'Yeah, well I fucking didn't. When's that grub going to be ready.'

'Not long now. So who were you on the Walker with? And did the B.M.C. cough up on the insurance for your rescue? Lynette told me that her mate Paula, who runs the scheme, had no record of any claim from you…'

'Look, I told you I can't remember, and I wasn't insured with the B.M.C. anyway—bunch of wankers!—now will you just leave it out. And as for Lynette, she told me you were a right twat, and to have nothing to do with you.'

Moss winced. His eyes flickered sideways, registered the hits he'd scored. He went back to tending the billy. They ate silently, Rigby refusing all eye-contact, the silence that rang between them through the long hours of night only broken by Rigby's snores and farts. In the brilliant light of morning Moss left Rigby making tea and sauntered along the shelf unroped. He shimmied on front-points along a smear of ice that led round a corner, and found himself on a rising terrace that gave a grandstand view of the other, western face of the mountain.

On this side the summit crest fell away in a near-vertical ice-slope below massive cornices for two thousand feet, before the angle eased and the slopes ran out into a hanging valley that was lumpy with debris from innumerable small avalanches. Far below the rim of the cirque, Moss could see a long, wooded gorge descending into the west—into the unknown, uncharted country on that side of the mountain.

'Far, far below, and hazy with distance, he could see trees rising out of a narrow, shut-in valley.'

Pushing up his snow-goggles for a minute, and squinting against the glare, he could make out the course of a sizeable river on the banks of which, far down, there were clearings in the forest. And before he pushed the goggles down again, he fancied he saw, even from this height, wisps of rising smoke.

'Or mist, more likely,' he muttered aloud, pondering to himself the likelihood of wood-cutters and herdsmen from across the great watershed having penetrated that far, or some unknown hill-tribe living there primitive and undisturbed. Whispering around the darkness of his mind there came stories their Sherpas had told—of *yetis* and *mi-gos*, *chumis* and *yilmus*, that came from the woods to seize

37

their yaks and children and women, driving or bearing them away into the trackless forests that surrounded the mountains; of a man captured by a female yeti, kept by her in a cave, with whom he'd conceived a son. After five years the man had escaped, taking the son with him, the Sherpas said, and that boy was of great strength and intelligence, was now the revered abbot at Kartaphu monastery. Had they been making fun of himself and Rigby with their ever-more-fantastic inventions, or was there some dim reality behind them?

'Who knows!' He laughed uneasily, and retraced his steps to the bivouac.

'Come on, mate—we're off in ten,' he snapped in response to the proffered mug of tea.

'What's it look like on that side?'

'Feasible. Dangerous. We need to get on it before the sun does. How d'you feel about moving unroped?'

'No,' came the swift response, 'bad idea—we might need the ropes if we find another way down...'

'If you lose bowel-control, more like,' thought Moss, and instead said 'OK then—but we need to be fast and if either of us falls, roped-up means one down, both down. Unless we use the old-fashioned safeguard.'

'What's that?'

'Throwing yourself off the other side of the ridge from the one who falls, and taking it from there—better in theory than practice.'

'Let's stay roped,' Rigby said, his voice high and sharp. They packed bivouac-tent and sleeping-bags away in their sacks, hefted them on their backs, tied on to either end of the ropes and Moss moved back round the corner on to the west face again.

'Shit!' Rigby gasped, as Moss indicated the line. 'If one of those cornices goes, we're frozen meat. Cold storage for eternity!'

'And the longer we hang around here, the more likely one will go.'

He led off, a slow waltzing progress across the smooth surface on front-points of his crampons, moving with a steady efficiency and a contained fearlessness under the curl and weight of cornices threatening from fifty feet above. When the full length of the ropes was run out, he placed a snow-anchor, hacked out a small platform, quickly brought Rigby across.

'Ten more of those and we're at the top.'

'And another ten coming back...'

'That's right, mate—spot on!'

'We should go down.'

'You can go down, but I'm not. It'll freeze again at nightfall and we can cross back by moonlight. Let's get the job done.'

'What about this trick of jumping down the other side?'

'You have to get on the ridge first—reckon you could do that faster than I'm falling?'

They had traversed another four rope-lengths, painfully slow progress with the sun rising to its zenith, Moss urging them on, impatience with his companion's awkward, slow progress eating at him and the snow-overhangs above softening and drooping into a long and curving esemplastic sequence, when chance tilted over into mishap. With a hiss and soft whoosh hundreds of tons of snow-ice fractured along the ridge-crest above Moss, slipped down on to him, and carried him away, gathering mass and momentum as it went.

A hundred horizontal feet away, Rigby had not even the time to untie from the rope, as he attempted, before it came taut and snatched him downwards. The dead-boy belay-plate from which he hung was plucked from its incision in the slope. It flew out into the sunlight that was now illuminating the face, glinting and whirling like some crazed mechanical toy whose motor-controls had defaulted to

39

chaos-mode before it disappeared into a roaring mist of ice-crystals.

'*…they fell a thousand feet, and came down in the midst of a cloud of snow upon a snow slope even steeper than the one above. Down this they were whirled, stunned and insensible, but without a bone broken in their bodies; and then at last came to gentler slopes, and at last rolled out and lay still, buried amidst a softening heap of the white masses that had accompanied and saved them.*'

Rigby, who had been catapulted down the slope when Moss's weight came on the rope, had fallen to one side of a brief, pinnacled spur in the lower section of the face. Their ropes had caught behind a *gendarme* and both men dangled from them as the avalanche swept over the lip of the hanging valley, scouring away the old avalanche debris, augmenting itself, doubling and trebling in size as it thundered into the ravine, snapping the first pines in its path as though they were no more than matchsticks. From their opposite sides of the little spur, lungs choking with ice, Moss and Rigby watched it pour on down and both of them shivered and yelled with the incredulous delight of still being alive.

As the blasting air and the roar receded, they took stock. One of Rigby's ice-axes hung from the sling by which he'd attached it to his harness at the belay. The other was gone. Moss had clung on to one of his throughout the fall, and by some quirk of kind providence the shaft of the other had speared into the snow right beside him on his side of the ridge. Even more miraculously, both men's rucksacks through that tumbling, cataclysmic descent had remained strapped to their backs.

As his head cleared of noise and disorientation, Moss checked his limbs. Nothing out of shape. Blood dripped on the snow. He felt his head. No helmet, and a sticky mess at the back of his scalp. He eased off a mitten and felt it gingerly. A scalp wound, tender, bleeding profusely, the skull beneath intact. He scooped snow and clamped it down to staunch the flow, pain burning through his consciousness.

'Joe…' he shouted, 'How are you?' And without waiting for a reply, cautiously he began to move up to the crest of their arresting spur, Rigby's weight causing the rope to run through its deep groove in the snow.

'Joe, get your weight off the rope!'

Rigby, startled by the sudden give in the rope, convulsed round, slammed his pick into the surface, and kicked his crampons into the slope. The rope now unladen, Moss reached the crest, coils of slack in his hand, and peered down.

'God! You look a mess!' Rigby jeered. 'How the fuck did we get away with that?'

'Guess you were right about the ropes—though we'd have been across and away without them.'

'Reminds me of when I took an involuntary trip down the Whymper Couloir on the Verte—two thousand feet and not a scratch on me…'

'Maybe I wouldn't have believed you before today. Anyway, tell me later. Let's get out of here before any more of those cornices come down.'

'Where are we heading?'

'Down—there's no way I'm going back up that slope in these conditions.'

'I thought you said it would freeze up again tonight?'

'How long, at our rate of progress, d'you think it would take us to get back to the level we were at—a day? Two days… And all the time the threat of more coming down, or the whole slope going with us on it? We've been lucky this time…'

'What about the Sherpas?'

'We'll see if we can get over a pass to the top of the Parasco glacier—it looked feasible on the aerial shots I saw —just head down that valley we can see and keep bearing left at the bottom. It should work, though from what I saw in the aerial shots, the topography in that area looked pretty complex. It's the place the Sherpas call the Seven Valleys—obviously loaded with significance for them. Nukku said his people would never go into that region, so we can't rely on them to come looking for us.'

'What about food?'

'We've enough for a few days if we go easy. We might find some below the tree line—fungi, bamboo shoots. And there'll be wood for fires.'

'How's your head?'

'Sore. But it's just a scalp wound. I'll live. I'm amazed I'm still living, after that.'

Towards dark on the following day, after a gruelling descent through the ice-fall beneath the hanging cwm, the two men reached the tree-line in the wide ravine below, made camp on a soft floor of pine needles with a glacier-melt stream running milk-white alongside, and collected wood for a fire. Thick disks of fungi adorned the trees. Moss collected some, cutting them off with his Swiss Army knife and dicing them into water in a billy that he put on the stove to boil.

'Trying to poison us?' asked Rigby, looking askance at the bloody mess.

'It's called beef-steak fungus, I think—I'm amazed to find it this high up, and on the wrong trees as well. It's not quite up to red-neck carnivore standard, but there's plenty of it, and it's edible enough. If we were back home I'd cut it in thin slices, fry it in butter with black pepper, and you'd think it a treat. It actually looks like steak. Weird stuff! Up here we'll have to make do with boiled. Shove in some rice and we'll have the perfect mushroom risotto.'

They ate—tentatively at first on Rigby's part—unrolled their sleeping bags by the fire, tossing on a few more branches for comfort and to keep the pre-moonrise darkness at bay, and settled down to sleep.

'Just like Shipton and Tilman, isn't it?'

'Yeah, but I hope we get better weather than they had wherever they went.'

'That was generally in the monsoon, daft buggers! We've a month yet before that's due to arrive. Should be enough time for another crack at Parasco if we make it back to base-camp sharpish.'

But Rigby made no reply.

By the time he awoke in the morning, Moss already had more mushroom risotto simmering on the stove and had prospected the route down-valley.

'I think there are bears up here,' he told Rigby, handing him a mug of tea, 'There are vague lines of paths between clearings. I went about half-a-mile down and it looks straightforward going. Good and bad news is that there are thickets of bamboo that might be hard to get through in the next vegetation zone down-valley. Change of menu for us there, though. Apparently Tilman thought they tasted like asparagus. Maybe we'll find an unknown colony of giant pandas and you can sell the story to *National Geographic*? 'How I fell down a mountain and found a colony of teddy bears?"

Moss allowed himself a smile at the thought of Rigby pitching to the commissioning editors. He carried on:

'There might be the odd nullah that's difficult to cross. We've ended up on the sunny side of the river and it looks as though there's a long sequence of grazing alps the whole way down to the confluence with the main valley down there. Left and left again up that, if I remember the photos right, and we'll be at the watershed for our glacier. It's unmapped, this bit of country—don't know of anyone having been in on this side of the mountain. There weren't any photographs apart from poor aerial ones and it was always assumed that the objective dangers were too much on this flank. Seems we've proved them right.'

They were leisurely about getting away, sitting round the re-kindled fire confident of their plan, recovering from the previous day's drama. Rigby even seemed to have divested himself for the moment of the need to recount endless suspect anecdotes, and was taking an interest in what was around him instead of seeking to impress by stories of what had—or had not—happened to him. Though his usual mode soon reasserted itself:

'Imagine if I'd broken my leg up there—tib-and-fib and the bone splinters out through the skin. And you'd been buried, no hope of getting you out. I could be like Doug crawling down from The Ogre, except I'd have written Clive out of the story if that'd happened to me. Instant best-seller, millions world-wide...'

Moss merely bestowed a long, levelling look on him of which Rigby remained unaware as he prattled on, story-telling, inventing or selecting the ingredients, even casting it as fictive dialogue between Moss and himself until the whole saga had grown into epic, primal stature.

They aired their sleeping bags in the morning sun, checked what provisions they had, collected some of the fungus lest food prove hard to find down-valley, drank several more brews and by ten o'clock had damped down the embers, covered over their fire-pit, packed their sacks and were away.

As Moss had predicted, at first their route led easily down from clearing to clearing, grassy and ablaze with flowers, idyllic among the pines. 'We're in Shangri-la,' Rigby said, a rare expression of relaxed happiness on his face. They sang and talked loudly as they went, to guard against the possibility of coming on a bear by surprise. When the descending contour line they followed along the valley-side reached the bamboo, they were surprised to find a trodden path leading through, and evidence of shoots having been gathered.

Rigby sang louder. Moss was thoughtful, looked carefully at the bamboo, at the path for prints of what might have been here. Around noon, on the farther side of the bamboo-zone, they stopped to make a brew of tea.

'There was something odd about the way the bamboo shoots had been taken. Did you notice? I don't think it's bears... They'd been cut, not bitten or broken off '

'Maybe it's the Yeti then,' Rigby came back. 'If so, we've hit the jackpot—you could name your own price with *National Geographic, Geo, Sunday Times* or wherever for that one. Get it syndicated. I'll be cruising out to Burbage in a Hummer come the autumn. Stuff your common-or-garden Range Rovers.'

'Not very eco-friendly of you, Joe,' Moss replied. Rigby looked at him to divine whether it was an amiable jibe or another of his ego-puncturing darts. But it was the intent direction of Moss's gaze that registered. He glanced over his shoulder and saw what had seized the older man's attention.

Walking towards them from the farther side of the clearing came two upright figures, moving easily and quickly and with obvious intent. Rigby reached for the ice-axe strapped to his rucksack.

'Put it down, Joe, and leave it down. Stay sitting.' Moss snapped. 'Show aggression and we're goners.'

'What do we do then?'

'We act calm and compliant and see what they want.'

'Suppose they want to eat us, like in the Sherpa stories?'

As they approached, Moss held eye-contact with the first of the men—for men they were. Both were well over six feet in height, deep-chested and powerfully-built, massive hands swinging by their sides as they strode over the grass. They were clad in loose trousers and smocks of rough-woven linen with broad woollen belts. Curious conical woollen head-dresses, reddish-brown in colour and with long ear-flaps, accentuated their height, and on their feet they wore rawhide pampooties with the big toe separate in its own sheath. Long auburn hair hung down in a plait from beneath their headgear, and their faces were tanned, high-cheekboned, with strong regular features and expressions of alert intelligence. Looking at them, Moss felt curiously calm and unafraid. Any threat, he felt, would come from their own behaviour.

Five yards away, the men drew to a halt. Moss held up his right hand in greeting, bowed his head and touched fingers to forehead, mouth and chest in one graceful movement, then turned the wrist and gestured with open palm for them to sit. They squatted one at either side as he poured the brew that had now come to the boil into the two mugs that were at the ready, and proffered one to each of the men. And as he did so, again with lowered head, he chanted this verse:

> *Asevanā ca bālānam*
> *panditānañ ca sevanāpūjā*
> *ca pūjanīyānametam.*

The cups were taken, sipped from appreciatively, and the elder of the two visitors inclined his head in acknowledgement.

'Do you practice these precepts of which you have sung?' he asked, in a deep voice, its inflection mocking and grave, his glance slipping lightly between Moss and Rigby, who was delving in his rucksack for a camera. 'Not to keep company with fools? To consort with the wise, and pay homage to the worthy—is this your creed, as it is ours? If so, you will be made welcome in our valley.'

As if by way of answer, Rigby had recovered from his open-mouthed astonishment at hearing their perfect English, taken his camera out, and was pointing it at the younger visitor, who reached out, took it from him, crushed it in one hand as though it were a ball of paper, and calmly, politely handed it back.

'Oh, fuck…' murmured Rigby, looking from man to mangled object in disbelief. Moss and the elder visitor exchanged a quick glance, the latter's stern demeanour flickering briefly into a smile that Moss returned with gratitude.

'We saw you come round the high slope of Parasco. By yourself, briefly, yesterday morning. We saw two of you crossing, high up beneath the ridge. You were foolish to have been there, moving so slowly. We saw the avalanche, and caused your rope to catch and arrest you.'

'You did what?' yelped Rigby, still chagrined at the loss of his camera. 'How could you do that?'

'Through thought,' the elder replied. The younger one continued in slow, emphatic tones. 'We have been aware of the disturbance—of your presence—since you first looked into this valley. Last night one of our lookouts kept watch nearby as you slept by your fire, making sure you brought no danger here.'

'So now,' the elder continued, 'you will come to the village. The elders will meet and talk with you before it is decided what to do. Take a last look at the way you have come, for you can never leave this valley now.'

And with that, he finished his tea, handed the cup back to Moss with an amused, stern inclination of his head, gestured the two climbers to make ready, and the party of four set off down-valley, Moss and Rigby walking together with their captors at a distance in front and behind.

'What d'you think he meant, 'We can never leave this valley now'?' Rigby asked.

'Just what he said, I imagine. And after the play with the camera, we're well advised not to disagree with them too immediately. You were pretty insensitive there. Besides, I rather take to them. And I'm fascinated to find out how they think they stopped our fall. Let's stay calm and go along with things. We could be in for a very interesting time here.'

'Yeah—and I could be losing a lot of money if I don't get back with this story—it's dynamite!'

'I doubt they allow dynamite in this valley, so you'd better just sit on it.'

'OK. And by the way, what the fuck were you saying to them when they arrived?'

'They translated what I said for you, if you were listening. It's from the *Mangala Sutta*—early Buddhist devotional text—I thought it might strike a chord with them. And anyway, it's been running through my mind continually since the avalanche.'

The way wound steeply down through stands of pine with alpine meadows falling away to the river on the right. Their guides—if that's what they were—kept up a tireless, fast, easy pace that soon had Moss and Rigby sweating in the sun. They stopped to take off windproofs and fleeces and stow them in their rucksacks, the guides halting for them to do so, but barely letting a glance wander in their direction.

'Suppose we made a run for it?'

'Try if you want and see where it gets you—I think we're going their way whatever, so best to give in gracefully. Besides, they know what we're thinking…'

'How d'you make that out?'

'I was watching the elder one as we talked. When he said that about causing the rope to catch, I wondered how developed their mental faculties were, so I tried a bit of simple telepathy.'

'What did you do?'

'I thought about a deer coming out of the forest to our right—didn't look that way, just watched his eyes. He looked. And when I made it change direction in my mind, he followed it on the ground. Except there wasn't an 'it', only in my imagination. Freaky or what! Still want to take your chances on making a run for it?'

A sharp descent brought them to a nullah swollen with afternoon snow-melt. It was twenty feet wide, deep and raging. The elder guide stepped back a pace, and in one bounding leap cleared it with ease. He took a stance on the farther bank and nodded to his younger companion, who pointed to Rigby's and Moss's rucksacks and held out his hand for them. They were tossed across as lightly as tennis balls, and after, picked up by scruff of neck and groin, sailed Rigby and Moss, to be fielded by the man on the farther side. Moss, who had been put down gently on grass, lay on his back and roared with laughter at the indignity of it, and the catcher nodded his head in amusement too. Something resembling a benign smile crossed his face. The last man made the leap look as easy as a short step.

'As I said, still want to make a run for it?'

'I guess not.'

They rounded the spur above the nullah, and a short descent through pasture where horned sheep grazed brought them into the village. Sixty or more houses were arranged in curving terraces below the forest-edge, looking out across the river. Balconies jutted out at first-floor level, sheltered by wide hanging eaves. They were solidly built of wood, with shingled roofs. Men dressed in the same flax suits and headwear as their guides, and women in vermilion-dyed skirts and brightly-embroidered blouses moved about their tasks. One huge figure worked a leather bellows smoothly up and down as his workmate plucked a bar of glowing metal from the forge and hammered at it on an anvil, sparks flying and the echoes of his blows travelling back from across the valley. Moss and Rigby felt like dwarves descended into a town of giants. Even the women were inches taller than either of them.

'Looks like we've hit Brobdingnag.'

'Yeah,' replied Rigby, not having a clue what he was on about.

They followed their guides down a main street where goats bleated and skipped away. Two dogs came up to Moss and Rigby, tails waving, sniffed at them, held up their muzzles in anticipation of affectionate caresses, and walked off with heads held high.

'Have you ever been in a Himalayan village as clean as this one, as orderly and well-built, as quiet? As sweet-scented? And even the dogs are benign. I think we've found ourselves a piece of civilization.'

'All I'm hoping for is the best restaurant west of Kathmandu,' said Rigby, 'and maybe a few beers to go with. Got your credit cards with you?'

The street led into a central concourse where wooden troughs brought water down from the mountainside to feed a stone-lined pool, within a low parapet, that seethed with large trout. A curiously-carved chair attached to a bar that tilted across a fulcrum hung above it, a ladder leading to the seat, the whole structure brightly painted in yellows and greens. On the same side of the pool, looking down on it, was a galleried bank of benches, the seat facing them. An air of calm pervaded the whole scene.

'No children,' mused Moss.

'They are in school at the lower village,' came the voice of the elder guide from behind him. 'These are the work-hours. The ones who live in this part of our settlement will be up here later. We have your rooms ready for you, but firstly you will take refreshment, and after the council of elders has met, we will explain your position to you. Sit here, please.'

A heavy pine table and several chairs had been placed on the terrace in front of the central house overlooking the concourse. Moss and Rigby eased off their rucksacks and took their seats, a guide on either side.

'Don't you guys have names?' Rigby enquired, chin jutting. 'It would make all this a whole lot easier. And by the way, how come you speak English, living right out here in the sticks?'

The elder guide flicked a dismissive glance at him and turned to Moss.

'We do not choose to bear names in our community. We are recognized by our occupations, our ages and parentage. This man is a carpenter, that one a shepherd; this woman shapes shingles for our roofs, those young men are cooks, that woman bakes bread; the woman up there coming out from the trees, she is the medicine woman, daughter of the old teacher. She gathers plants and herbs from the forest. You might call her our professor of botany.'

The shadow of a smile that haunted his face gleamed briefly.

'She will treat your head-wound in due course. I have told of what you would need.'

'But you haven't spoken to her yet,' retorted Rigby in a jeering tone, gratified at having caught him out.

'Your friend has already noticed that we communicate by thought, and has informed you of this fact. Your understanding is slow.'

Turning to look at Rigby, he continued, his demeanour less warm and confiding: 'You have seen the smiths at their forge. From childhood, natural gifts are recognized, skill and knowledge developed from those. All within our community know their own and each others' roles. There is no need for naming to set each other apart. You, Rasselas Moss, and you, Joseph Rigby, have no further need of those appellations and the baggage they carry. You are no longer of that time, but of this place now, and must adapt. I now have to report to the council of elders. You will meet with them later. Food and drink is being prepared for you. Please eat and relax.'

With an inclination of his head to Moss, he walked off into the house behind them.

'So where did you come by the daft moniker, and how the fuck did you come to know that, what did you call it?—Mangra Sutra. What is it anyway?'

'Same reason as what you choose to call my 'daft moniker'. That came from my parents. It's after Johnson's little Utopia novel. They taught me the *Mangala Sutta*—as I told you back there, it's an early Buddhist devotional text, a kind of discourse on blessings and right behaviour—as well. It had taken over from the Christian gospels for them as they grew older.'

'They're still alive, then…'

'No—they died in a car crash in India. My mother was a doctor and my father was a missionary to the Khasi tribes up in Meghalaya. They'd gone out there after I started at uni—something they'd always talked of doing. Didn't factor Indian roads and drivers into the equation, I suppose.'

From the house into which their guide had disappeared, the three young men he had pointed out emerged. Now wearing long aprons, carrying trays of food. They placed on the table bowls of saffron rice and of ladies' fingers, dishes of dhal and of potato boiled then fried with aromatic methi. Platters of unleavened bread glistened with ghee in front of Moss and Rigby. They returned with a tall silver teapot and small, unglazed terra cotta cups. One of the young men poured out milky *chai* into the cups, handed them one each.

'Please, eat…'

The tallest of the young men gestured with open palm at the food before them, and withdrew into the house. Rigby took a sip from his cup and grimaced.

'Fucking goat's milk! Tastes like my socks after I've worn them a month. I suppose you're the sort of macrobiotic old hippy who lives off the stuff…'

'I'm not that keen,' said Moss, as Rigby scanned the table and began to pile food into the bowl placed before him, spooning potato into his mouth, wiping the sauce in which the okra had been stewed from his stubble with a piece torn off one of the naan breads. Moss watched with the old, fastidious distaste rising again, and knew that this too was an aspect of their presence now being discussed in the elders' council. He brought his hands together, touched them to his forehead—conscious as he did so of Rigby's leering disapproval—and took sparingly from each dish. Rigby too refilled his bowl, wolfed it down rapidly, belched loudly and pushed his chair away from the table:

'Not bad! Not up to lamb balti standards at the Mysore on Eccleshall Road though. I could really go for a pint or two of Carlsberg now. Wonder if there's any alcohol in this place…'

'Something tells me there isn't. Want a bit more from the *Mangala Sutta*?'

'Go on then if you must, but with a translation this time…'

> *'To abhor and avoid all evil,*
> *Abstention from intoxicants,*
> *And diligence in righteousness.*
> *This is the most auspicious sign.'*

'Well whoever's auspices those are, I don't fancy living under them.'

'Doesn't look like you've got a choice in the matter.'

'How did you know they were Buddhists, anyway?'

'I didn't, and I don't. We're just talking behavioural precepts, and they're into those clear as day.'

'It all sounds a bit corn-cob-up-your-arse to me. I'd sooner Irvine Welsh, personally speaking.'

'See yourself as Sick Boy then…'

'Back off—you're no Renton.'

'That's for sure. Look—here comes our friend again…'

'More your friend than mine, I reckon.'

'I'd work on it if I were you.'

Their guide came out from the house behind them, walked across the terrace and joined them at the table.

'You have enjoyed your food?'

Moss made the same flowing gesture from forehead to mouth to heart, and the guide studied him carefully.

'Good, I am glad,' he nodded. 'I will show you your room,' he said to Rigby, and to Moss, 'You stay here—someone will come to tend to your head.'

He stood and gestured Rigby to follow. They descended steps from the terrace, entered a house three doors down the street, climbed stairs to first-floor level and the guide opened a heavy wooden door into a plain room with a table, a chair, and an open cupboard on to the shelves of which the contents of Rigby's rucksack had been incongruously unpacked. A narrow sleeping-couch covered in woven blankets was pushed against one wall, and a door led on to a small balcony overlooking the concourse.

'You will be brought water for bathing. The necessary offices are through here...'

He opened another door towards the rear of the room, through which was a hanging alcove on the back wall of the house, in it a bench seat with a hole in it, a basin and a ewer alongside.

'The pigs from the forest eat your evacuations, for which reason we do not eat the pigs,' the guide explained in response to Rigby's quizzical look.

With that he left the room, shutting the door quietly behind him, and returned to join Moss on the terrace. The woman they had seen earlier coming out of the forest was standing beside him. His chair was facing away from the table and his head was tilted back over a bowl of water. She was washing the blood out of his hair, and inspecting the long, ragged split in his scalp. She considered it carefully, massaging his scalp gently as she did so.

'We must sew this now,' she breathed at him. 'If I could have done this yesterday it would have been better...'

From the bag she had with her, she took a bobbin wound with thread, and a curved needle. She picked him up with his chair as easily as if he were a small child, turned him back to the table, dried the wound with a linen cloth, pressed its edges together and sewed them deftly, snipping the thread away after each suture with a small pair of scissors.

When the sewing was complete, she took from her bag an oilskin package, produced out of it a pad of brilliant green sphagnum, placed it on the wound with a pad of linen above, and proceeded to bandage up the whole with long linen strips secured round his forehead and running diagonally behind his skull. Moss remained perfectly quiet and submissive throughout the process and the guide looked on silently. The woman finished her work, packed her bag and withdrew back into the house. The guide reached across, touched Moss's elbow, and said, 'Come.' They followed her inside, climbed stairs and Moss was shown into a larger and lighter version of Rigby's room.

'Rest well. We will talk in the morning. The council of elders will see you then.'

Moss undressed and pulled aside the covers on his bed. There were clean sheets of coarse linen, a long roll of pillow at the head. He climbed in and within seconds was deeply asleep.

He woke early to the bleating of sheep and goats, and a metallic hammering. He wrapped himself in a blanket and stepped out on to the balcony. By the forge one of the smiths was beating a sheet of heated brass into a cylindrical shape, using Moss's hammer-axe. Its nylon-tape leash was wrapped round his brawny wrist, and from time to time he held the implement up, studying it, appreciating its fine balance and workmanship. He looked up, saw Moss watching, and waved the tool at him with a broad grin. 'Good!' he shouted down the street, and returned to his work.

Two young shepherds were driving a flock of skipping sheep and bounding goats through the concourse and on towards the pasture-land that lay beyond the village. The valley was filled with mist. Parasco was a dark silhouette at the valley-head against a deep blue sky. Villagers were already out on the streets, busying themselves about their daily tasks, and a group of children bustled along a path heading down-valley, chanting musically in high, piercing voices as they went.

His elder guide from yesterday was sitting at the table on the terrace with the herb-woman, a teapot between them. He turned his head to Moss and gestured to him to come down.

The woman poured him *chai*, stood behind him and ran her hands over the dressing on his skull. He winced, despite the gentleness of her touch. She reached round and caught hold of his chin, turned his face towards her, opening the lids of his right eye wide and peering intently into the pupil. A glance passed between her and the guide. She adjusted his dressing and took a seat beside him, turned his hand palm upwards and felt his pulse. Moss, discomfited by the intimacy, looked to the guide:

'Is Rigby awake yet?'

'Awake, yes,' responded the guide, 'but not here. He left in the night. His room is empty.'

'You know where he's gone?'

'Yes, of course—he intends reaching your camp on the glacier beyond Parasco. He will not make it.'

'D'you mean you will stop him?'

'There is no need for us to do that. When I told you that you can never leave this valley, my meaning was not that we shall hold you captive. It is the land will do that.'

'So do you never leave it?'

'There is a way out that we know—the crooked way by the Spirit Bridge. We use it to reach the trading place with the Bhotias, by Kartaphu seven valleys away, each spring and autumn. Even if Rigby could find it, he could not pass it without our assistance. This is why we have remained here untroubled for so many centuries.'

'So what can Rigby do?'

'He may die, or he may return—the choice is his.'

'Do you mean to find him, to help him return…'

His guide's unflinching gaze gave him the answer.

'Might I go, to help him back? He must have some chance of being helped back, surely?'

'We are not a penal colony here. He chose to attempt to leave, despite our warning. We cannot regret his departure, his presence being a pollution here. The probability now is that he will die. See where the gorge turns north…'

Moss peered down-valley and the topography for the first time began to register. A long ridge thrown out to the west from the southern summit of Parasco that Moss and Rigby had reached suddenly curved round, the dip slope on the valley side of it channelling the river into a shadowy gorge.'

'…and the other side of that ridge?' queried Moss.

'Only the eagles can pass there.'

Moss didn't even trouble himself to enquire after the gorge. His eyes searched the wooded, nullah-seamed slopes. They fell from a bounding ridge that buttressed Parasco's main summit and curved round towards the ravine.

'Yes, said the guide, 'our trading path is there. When you have accepted your destiny, you will come with us perhaps…'

'And today may I go to find Rigby and bring him back?'

'You would already be too late. He is in the gorge now. Reality is leaving him. Through his stories, he has convinced himself that he can master all obstacles. This has been their purpose in his life, as I'm sure your compassion informed you. But those tales took place only in his imagination—your suspicions about them were well-founded. Only fools and the sensation-seekers of your

57

society would have been taken in by them. He is now about to make the last decision preceding his death. You do not have the strength to help him. There is a fever coming on you. Drink as much of the tea as you can. It will help. Do not eat. Then return to your bed. This woman will care for you through your illness. She is very skilled.'

Aware of his head throbbing and heat coursing through his body, he looked beyond his guide and asked about the seat-and-bar structure above the pool in the concourse.

'When we first came to this valley, hunted with spears and knives and poisoned darts out of the plains by superstitious fear among the numerous tribes who lived there, it was necessary for us to banish negativity and hatred from our people's minds. At first we were primitive in how we accomplished this. We thought it could be done by force and punishment. Those who transgressed in word or action, who expressed hatred or intended harm to others, were strapped into the chair and lowered into the pool. We anointed their eyelids with pig-fat from animals we had fed to the dogs beforehand, to signify their way of seeing. The fish would eat away this thin veil of polluted flesh. When they came from the water, their eyes were forever opened. They would be scourged, and driven into the forest, where the bears and wild pigs would kill and devour them. We have not used the machine in this way for many years. As you can see, the fulcrum has been disabled...'

He mused for a moment, before he went on:

'It was mentioned last night at the council, however, that Rigby might benefit from our ducking-stool. But the suggestion was not serious, and you may take it as an example of our humour. We use it now as the seat of witness for those who appear before council. It stands as a monument to our past cruelties, reminding us of the need for charitable understanding. '

'Who are you, then? Who are your people?'

'The hill-tribesmen call us *yeti*. They are deeply afraid, tell outlandish stories of our behaviour and appearance, talk childishly of how we eat their people, of how offensive and rank is our smell. These are the kind of untruths that are born of fear and misunderstanding—you will know that from your society. Take this woman's hand, put it to your nostrils, and experience the sweetness of it…'

Moss looked to her in embarrassment. With a mocking smile she stretched out her hand to his face, he held it and breathed deeply of the smell of her skin, sweet with herbs for which he had no name. Clean, fine hairs were pale against her deeper tan, her skin unlined. His eyes followed up the smooth musculature of her arm and met hers, their irises a bright, clear amber. A moment's intense connection and she withdrew her hand, looked back to his guide with a smile.

'So you are the *yetis*…'

'Not in our own language—only in the words of the foolish.'

'Why are you here?'

'I have told you something of how we came here. But perhaps it is of our purpose in this world that you enquire? We were the unfallen ones, who sought enlightenment. The people who then lived in the world drove us out, fearing for their possessions, for their pleasure, their pride; envious of our gifts. We were guided to this place, which is the pure land.'

'Guided by who?'

The guide touched fingers to forehead, lips and heart.

'You will learn. But you must rest now. When you have come through the ordeal of your fever and are recovered, the elders will welcome you and arrange for you to learn all you might wish to know. You will be well cared for here…'

'What of Rigby?'

'He took his last breath as we talked. It has bubbled out and merged with the foam of the rapids. That is as far as he could approach to unity. The Ghost River is taking him down though the whirlpools of Jun, out to the Yellow Springs and the Region of the Dead. You will not follow him there. Your journey is a different one and your body will lie eventually in our Sacred Grove. I have not yet told you of the man who was known to your people as Nunez. He was the last to come here over Parasco. He has lived with us for many years. His son is the young Rinpoche at Kartaphu, and is known there as Gyaltsen. In time your son will succeed him. This is how we ensure the vital and healthy continuance of our tribe and the race to which we both belong. It will be explained to you. Rest now…'

'A gift to their gene pool—is that how they view me, and viewed Nunez? How did he come here? Is he still alive, I wonder? And what did happen to him on Parasco? If he made that ascent, it was surely the greatest in mountaineering history. Thank heavens Rigby didn't meet him; otherwise there'd have been another tall and borrowed tale for the retelling. But how did he get down…'

The questions raced round his head as the woman led him back to his room, helping him in his weakness up the stairs, undressing him and bathing his body as though he were her child, and his head whirled and swam as though he himself were struggling for his life where the river turned north and plunged thousands of feet down into the gorge that was as fearsome as it was impassable.

For five days he thrashed and groaned in the grip of high fever, his body a maze threaded through with scintillating pain, burning, parched throat gasping, the woman in her majestic strength and beauty always by him, supporting him to drink, bathing him with cool water, placing him on the copper bed-pan to relieve himself, holding the basin into which he vomited continuously until his stomach muscles yearned away from the need to retch again. His dreams were a wild confusion, wayward and inexplicable, palpable but at a remove from reality, in a realm of psychogenic torment.

Rigby came to him, transformed from mundane reality as obstreperous bully and fantasist to something red and horned, raging against him and seeking his destruction, spewing out scalding jealousies, fork-tailed and diabolical as any creature of corbel-table carving that jetted the contents of gutters out on to graveyards he remembered from wondering childhood. Their weird forms crowded and danced through his imagination, danced across slabs and tombs beneath which his x-ray vision saw skeletons squirm in their coffins and rattle their dry bones. What demons are these, he screamed? All stilled for a second, ominously. Yet again Rigby burst out like a great leaping fish from the whirlpools of Jun, skin as deadly white as that of the corpse-whale, brandishing a rattle-bag of stories in his wrinkling hand, reaching into it frantically time and again to pull out a new tale and begin its telling, only for the smug self-glorifications he evoked to fade from definition and disperse into a cold glitter of dew that dripped from dead branches on to his diminishing dark hunched and scowling figure.

'All true, all true,' he shrieked, as each narrative evaded him. Moss held out a hand to comfort him, but he shrank from it, his skin like putty, his voice changing to a pleural gurgling and then silence as he plunged back into the swirling dark water, his face a paleness sinking, sinking. The ice-peaks Moss had trodden were red-stained and dancing along every holding horizon of his thought and the world swayed continually, its planes shifting, dizziness scouring all clarity from his mind. Pain and pandemonium in his brain built to the point where it was on the verge of cracking his skull. Words in clotted gouts of hard-uttered sentences spilled headlong hysterically out of his slack and drooling mouth, the woman wiping away hanging elastic threads of saliva and jade rivulets of trickling bile as he recited his passionate remembered mantra:

'*A floodtide of screaming fiends and assassins and thieves and hirsute buggers pours forth into the universe, tipping it slightly on its galactic axes. The stars go rolling down the void like redhot marbles. These simmering sinners with their cloaks smoking carry the Logos itself from the tabernacle and bear it through the streets while the absolute prebarbaric mathematick of the western world howls them down and shrouds their ragged biblical forms in oblivion.*'

Rigby's ghastly face once more broke surface, the pleural bubblings shaping themselves into angry jeering utterance:

'Where the fuck's that from, then, know-it-all? Not more of your *Mangala Sutta*? Not more of that pretentious shit, is it? Why d'you bother with that inflated crap?'

Moss was laughing. 'No,' he wailed, 'It's Cardinal McCarthy's *Suttree Sutta* on beneficence—recite it and even you are forgiven. Among the liars and the low and the lush and the lascivious. You can be forgiven. Joe! Joe! Come back!' and he turned to the woman and grasped her arm shuddering as Rigby sank again into whirlpool depths, last bubbles of air from his drowned lungs shaped by his dumb mouth into its final expression, rising and bursting at the surface into indifferent air. Other words came echoing out of his memory, solemn chantings, clouds of incense wreathing around them as the black figures shrank into their chasubles and swung the censers, processing with sinister power down the aisle, glaring from side to side for souls to drag into purgatory. Moss knelt at the end of a pew, cringing away as one priest turned towards him. His erect member was lifting cassock and alb, his free and bony hand pressing Moss's face down to take it blue-veined and stinking into his mouth. Nicotinous fingers, death's-head peering down, the creak of chains, the wafting smoke, his boy-self choking at each priestly thrust. 'No!' he cried, and the priest cried louder, 'Yes, yes, oh yes…!' as the others intoned:

'Miserere mei, Deus, omnis malignia discordia…'

Lynette too writhed in his mind, fleshy and warm, the musk of her body pervading his senses as she twisted and snaked through his dream, her body coiling and thrashing around him, breasts flailing against his cheeks with a loud slapping sound, her kisses swallowing him down, pubic bone hard against his thigh, her vulva agape to envelop him like the Sheelagh-na-gig at Kilpeck where they had stopped at her insistence one summer's evening, on a long detour vaguely homewards after a weekend of fierce first ascents on Stackpole Head with the great waves washing and surging past beneath; and in that round and pagan churchyard peaceful under a westering sun she had slipped into her recline on dewy grass and pulled him down on her. 'My pleasure now,' she had gasped, wet with desire, clinging to his hair and bucking against him as he thrust into her. His febrile brain entered into the quiet memory of that peaceful border place with the forest ridges rolling across blue with twilight into Wentwood and the hill of dreams to the south, and as suddenly as he knew himself there the fever passed and he lay quieted at last on the bed, his breathing regular, limbs stilled, his eyes shut at last.

The woman from the forest stood up, looked down on him with a smile and crossed over to the window. She beckoned to her daughter who was working in the twilight at the table below, tying herbs into bundles for drying. Moss heard as if from another world the younger woman mount the stairs and enter the room, but his eyes were fast shut and his consciousness spilling down into an exhausted sleep.

After a brief embrace from which both drew back to look the other questioningly in the face, the two women walked hand-in-hand to the bed. The woman of the forest handed Moss over into her daughter's care and walked away spent and drawn to her own chamber, where she undressed, unfastened the braids from her hair, climbed into bed and sank with a grateful sigh into its quiet, solitary relief.

Moss awoke to morning light flooding into the room. He looked up and saw his guide and the younger woman standing by the bed watching him. The man caught his quizzical expression.

'My daughter…' he explained, turning to the young woman with a smile.

'Then you and the woman from the forest are man and wife?' Moss whispered from a dry throat.

'We do not have marriage here as you would know it, but we are united as parents of this child. In this place, unity is all.'

The young woman blushed.

'Father, I am now twenty-one. I have passed beyond childhood.'

'You have, Daughter. And you must forgive a father's memories that hold you back from your womanly destiny.'

He turned to Moss again. 'You are strong and resilient, my friend, and I think you are able to come to our council today. You will be brought food and drink, and water to bathe. Clothes have been made for you by our tailors. Ready yourself, and I will return soon to escort you to the meeting of the elders.'

With that, he and the young woman walked from the room. Moss lay back on the bed and mused on the calm presence of father and daughter: on the strength and fine features, the uncanny insight of the man, and the dignity and extraordinary beauty of the woman, in whom the merits of her parents seemed to him perfectly refined and expressed.

As he was conjuring her to his thoughts again, the door opened and she entered, followed by the three young men who had brought food to him and Rigby when they had arrived a week before. One man carried a large bowl and pitcher of water, and a towel over his arm. The other men put plates of flat breads, dishes of apricots, honey, yogurt and cheese on a low table by the bed, a teapot and a single cup with them. Then all three withdrew.

Alone with him, the woman, venturing a shy glance at Moss, took the clothes she was carrying on her arm, placed them on the end of his bed, and held them up one by one. An undershirt and drawers of fine, unbleached linen—she blushed and smiled as she showed them to him. A long shirt of heavy, soft cotton; the same kind of loose trousers and smock that the guides had worn when Moss and Rigby had first met them; and a braided woollen belt dyed a vivid green. She laid them out on the bed, along with thick woollen socks and a pair of the rawhide pampooties, and with a smile and a toss of her auburn hair and a nod that he might have taken as challenge or mockery, she glided across to the door and left him alone in the room.

'Whatever I'm being prepared for, they're showing kindly intent,' he mused, then made a gesture of thankfulness and addressed himself to the first food he had eaten in days.

An hour later, washed and dressed, he made his way on to the terrace, where the guide waited. Benches on the galleried bank were filling up with the elders of the village, men dressed in the same clothes he now wore, women in skirts and embroidered bodices, both sexes wearing the conical woollen head-dresses, long braids of hair hanging beneath them, many still of the deep auburn hues of his guides and the herb-woman and her daughter, others white-haired, their faces all with expressions of benign concentration and expectancy.

'Come,' said his mentor, strong hand supporting his elbow, 'you must take the seat of inquisition now.'

He led him over to the structure above the pool, helped him climb the ladder into the carved seat on the bar. 'No need to strap you in, I think—none here view you as felon or threat.'

With that, he walked across and took his place on the first and lowest row of benches. Looking up at the faces ranged above him, Moss thought of the small theatres throughout Britain where he'd lectured to rapt audiences about his mountain exploits. And a sense of relief flooded him that he would never have to go through those posturing charades again; resort to the formulaic understatements that were in fact a kind of ironic boastfulness; provide proxy thrills to those hungry for vicarious sensation. He stood at the gate of a new life, and with a mind as perfectly emptied as it had been in those moments before the crux on any of his hardest climbs, he felt a kind of joy in anticipation.

A small flock, the size of thrushes, swished past to settle twittering and singing on the roof of a barn on the hillside just below. The elders' eyes followed them. An old man, still upright and tall, stood up and stepped forward a few paces to stand in front of Moss. At his right hand a woman, equally dignified, accompanied him, and on his left a shorter man of powerful, stocky physique and a complexion swarthier than the burnished villagers, his hair of darker hue too, its curls grey flecked.

'We welcome you, friend, to our fortunate place,' the old man began. 'This valley has been our refuge for many centuries, and we have mindfully sustained ourselves here and kept our race vigorous through the traditions that were handed down to us. Our purpose here is that of maintaining a pure human stock against any disaster that may befall so-called mankind through its own base tendencies.'

He halted, aware of a troubled look on Moss's face. In the latter's mind a bright warning notice had flashed. It read 'Eugenics!' Moss looked round the assembled faces and saw the concerned smiles on all of them.

'We understand what is meant by this term,' the old man continued. 'It is not our way. The path we follow in striving for the better state is one that seeks to remedy the negative tendencies of the mind. You will have many questions around this, and the friend here at my left hand, who came to us forty years ago in the manner you have now done, will seek to answer them, and to instruct you further in the ways of our people. He and the guide who brought you here…'

The old man half-turned and gestured to Moss's host.

'…these two men, and this woman here, who is mother to the Rinpoche of Kartaphu…'

He took the hand of the woman on his right and raised it in salutation to Moss.

'…they will be your mentors and instructors. Through talk with them, you will find your place and your role here. Your arrival here is a happy one for us. We trust it will be so for you to. Because you have been so ill, we will not prolong this present audience with our council, among which in time you too will surely sit.

'For the present, this is now your home and can provide all you need. You may go wherever you like—all is held in common here, and your teachers will explain our customs. Tomorrow you will begin to accompany them on the path, and your own heart too, in which we trust, will act as a guide. Serenity will come to you here. You are far away now from the commotion and threat of the world in which you have long lived, which must change before it destroys itself.

'Your good fortune is to have fallen into the fortunate place. The attempt to leave it destroyed your former companion, though he may yet return purged in another cycle of existence. You—as are all of us here—have assumed your final incarnation. You journey now into the realm of spirit, of the great symbols, and know already something of its rigour. Friend, we wish you luck and a pure mind.'

With that, the entire body of those present stood up, gave Moss the flowing gesture of salute from forehead to lips to heart, and filed slowly away into the village or the fields. The old man who had spoken turned away and followed them, and his two companions stood at either side of the ladder to help Moss from his seat. He walked a little shakily back up the steps to the terrace with the man and woman supporting him on either side. They sat at the table and a young man brought tea.

'So you once were Nunez?' Moss asked of the man.

'Yes, and today we may talk of that by council's dispensation as a means to the exorcizing of your past.'

'You did what I failed to do, in reaching the summit of Parasco.'

'You will soon learn not to think in these relative terms. After my companion chose to retreat, I climbed on for a little way, intending soon to follow him down. Through that act of faith I received the mountain's gift. You too have known moments like this. What I believe is called a trap-dyke by those who study rocks, filled with perfect snow, led me without difficulty to the summit. I shouted to Pointer, but he had already descended beyond earshot. And I was glad. I realized in that instant that I was at liberty, and once on the summit the mountain gave a further gift. Our expedition had already discounted the south ridge that you climbed…'

'How on earth did you know that?' Moss blurted, regressing for a moment to his old consciousness.

'You know how I know, and enough of that. What we did not know on our expedition, and nor did you, was of the west ridge from the high summit of Parasco—the ridge that leads down into these woods above us here.'

Nunez gestured towards the forest beyond the village houses.

'It was before me that day forty years ago, I saw that it was perfectly straightforward, as no-one else had ever done because access to its foot is complex and difficult—to reach it you would have to trek through the Seven Valleys —and no nearby peak overlooks that side of the mountain.

By the time I had reached the tree-line on the descent the sun was setting...'

'My god, you must have been fit...'

The dark man allowed himself a rueful smile, and carried on:

'I came across a path that I assumed had been made by animals, started to follow it down, sat down for a moment to rest, and two guides from the village greeted me as they did you not many days ago.

'That is how I came here. What will be of more interest to you now is what I have learned through being here.'

'Would you tell me of that?'

'I will give you its essence—the rest you will come to know over many years, through study, and labour, and love. The essence is unity. All the lessons you have so far intuited lead to that goal. This is why we have no names, no possessions but those held in common, no desire but for the good of all. You are twenty-six years old, the age I was when I arrived here forty years ago. You have come to the point in your life where you are receptive to these truths, and the place where they may flourish. The Buddhists would call the state to which your heart now yearns that of the bodhisattva...'

'Are you then Buddhists here? I had wondered about that...'

'Buddhism is a name; with all the perils that naming brings in the spiritual realm. Names can be claimed by those unworthy of them. We are wary in our awareness. Also, our role is as the reservoir of an unpolluted human stock. All that might jeopardize this destiny is put aside by us.'

'You are a kind of chosen people then?'

Nunez flashed a quick admonitory look at him.

'To believe that would be spiritual pride, spiritual materialism. Though we seek to live well, we do not claim to be better than others. The relative, by definition, is a place of dispute. Far away and long ago, when I was growing up on the borders of France and Spain within sight of La Rhune, the turmoil those attitudes caused even as a child was apparent to me. So I sought out the realm of impersonal conflict that is another of the mountain's gifts. In common with you, my friend…'

The two men's eyes met and held each other's gaze for long seconds before Nunez carried on speaking.

'In the summer in which I came to the fortunate valley, a young tulku from Surmang monastery, fleeing to the west before the Chinese forces, passed through here. How he found his way is not important—things happen as they are meant to happen, gates open, ways become clear. He became the Rinpoche Chogyam Trungpa, and as you know he ended his life as drunkard and debauchee across oceans in the far cold west—how does your old Yorkshire rhyme go? *From Hell and Hull and Halifax the lord deliver us?*

'Though he had been seeking to found the kingdom of Shambhala, this Rinpoche created his own hell in the other Halifax across the ocean. Had he paused only to reflect, undazzled by the admiration of his followers and the confusion of needing to challenge them, surely he would have known that Shambhala is always within. Like hell, it too is of our own creating.'

Moss searched his memory for two lines from a Christina Rossetti poem:

> *'It may be, could we look with seeing eyes,*
> *This spot we stand on is a Paradise?'*

'Yes, your poet has it exactly right, and our young Rinpoche, in the confusion of his flight, did not *look with seeing eyes*. He was a proponent of *yeshe cholwa*—the crazy wisdom. I do not think the peace and rigour of our community appealed then to his young mind. He went west, and spread a message of sorts among people without

70

the rigour fully to heed its implications. But I must hold back from lack of charity in my judgement here. And you must learn for yourself, as I did from my first years.

'Though you are young, you have made much progress already in your life, and the time was proper for you to come here. You had already learnt that to hate an abstraction—be it injustice, cruelty, abuse of power—is permissible; but to hate another living creature is a curse against your own spirit, and puts you in thrall to evil.

'Your guides recognized this in you before they led you here. They knew it of me too, from my time in Spain. We have been lucky, as your friend Rigby was not. The whirlpools of Jun are a centrifuge, will spin what's weak and wicked out of him before his time comes to set forth once more on the journey.

'Now, I must talk to you of practicalities. There is little need here for your former calling as language teacher. We have the ability to intuit all modes of speech, all languages —what is known elsewhere as the gift of tongues.

'All those in our community work the land, and we are blessed in its goodness, in the gentleness of our climate. Also, you may try any other task until the one to which your gifts are suited becomes plain. My work is with wood, from the planting and growing of trees to cutting timber for building or heating our houses or shaping bowls for our table, and to making charcoal for our metal-workers to use in smelting the silver, copper and iron we have here in plenty.

'Your guide, who lives in the house where you will continue to stay, keeps watch over our community, observes travellers, directs the journeys of the lost and brings to our community those we need for its continuity and health. But all who join us do so willingly. It is not, as you thought, an experiment in eugenics…'

Nunez finished speaking, and after moments of reflection, Moss posed a question:

'Yet those who arrive here cannot leave, and presumably must participate?'

'If they wish to leave, our professor of plants—she who resides in the same house as you, and tended to you in your illness—will administer a draught of forgetfulness that she prepares with utmost care from a poisonous forest plant that we call *bikh*—you will know it as aconite. After they have swallowed this, they are guided through the Seven Valleys to our trading post, and Lobsang of the Bhotias arranges their passage from there.

'But they may never come back, having made that decision; and they will never know happiness again after leaving this place.'

A verse from Rumi ran through Moss's mind:

> *'Do not expect your heart to return.*
> *When it dissolves in love,*
> *It is gone for good.'*

He recited it. His interlocutor nodded and smiled.

'Tell me,' asked Moss, 'of how it is between the men and women in this place?'

Nunez studied him for a moment, then lowered his eyes, talking fast and seriously.

'We all must master the importunities of desire, but we do not expect that this should inflexibly be the case throughout all phases of our lives. Also, our community must be sustained as safeguard against humanity's capacity for self-destruction.

'Our women may each bear one child in their lifetime. The woman, when she is of age, chooses the man by whom she would breed, tells her mother of her choice, and the mother approaches the man. These bargains are made for life, and fleshly contact between the man and woman takes place at the proper times and in the allotted place until she is with child.

'Then their time of physical union remains between them as the sweetest of memories, the foundation of fondness, and is never revisited, nor does either desire that it should be. Memory of it is enshrined in the honorific, used uniquely between such pairs of 'My Dear One'.

'The unity of the community is our bond. You know from your western society how destabilizing, how destructive, is the power and mystery of sexual union. Here all is put at service of the common good. Unity in community is our way.

'All that threatens that, we have dispensed with. There is no jealousy, no possessiveness here, no competition, with all the rage and disturbance that brings in its wake. The woman makes her choice. The child of their union is brought up, knowing its parents, by the whole community. The friendship between its parents is lifelong and unthreatened, unimpeachable.

'You yourself will soon be absorbed into this process, and thus become a member of our community, and it will bring you lasting peace of mind. You will know the joy, in all its aspects, of becoming one.'

'And if the child should die, may they try again?'

'No child has died in this valley through the centuries since our community arrived. This is a blessed and fortunate place, where the spirits watch over us. Our lineages are assured. My son, as you know, is Rinpoche at Kartaphu. For me and for his mother, my Dear One, you have arrived to take his place and salve our natural sorrow at separation. If a member of our community leaves to enter a monastic community or to perform good works elsewhere in the world, providence always fills the gap thus left, and strengthens our line. '

'What is the purpose of the silent mode of communication you practice here. Is it what we from outside would call telepathy, or thought-transference?'

'Not transference, but the ability to read what is in another's mind. It is one of many instinctive modes those in the west once possessed in fuller measure, and have now almost entirely lost. The incipient power is there in you, as you demonstrated to your guide with the pictures of the deer by which you tested him.

'Its purpose we see as this: if everyone can see your thoughts, the incentive to keep them pure is hence very great. So it becomes in itself the best guard against the prevalent sickness in your society of malevolent projection. Where all are as one, and all is known, the temptation to revile is absent. We do not practice calumny in this place.'

'Do you have no sense here in this valley of the malignant demons that haunt the minds of those who live in the societies from which you and I both came?'

'Why would we want to have brought those creatures of darkness with us? The demons are those who always deny and decry, whose quality of being can find expression only in negativity. When we come to see these mendacious ones as they truly are, they lose all power to harm and must slink away ashamed.

'Think of those in the societies of which we have spoken who seek their physical gratification with the innocent, with children. Think of the loathsome whisperings as they practise their corrupt seductions: the stepfather who urges on his Dear One's daughter that 'this will be our little secret, that your mother mustn't know about'. The priest who extends the power of confidentiality held by the confessional box to conceal his own perverse pleasures. The teacher with whom you would not wish to be left behind in a classroom. The lecturer who gives high marks in return for physical favours. The powerful woman who assumes those men of rank and status below her own to be her play-things. The famous who prey on those who desire proximity to fame.

'The problems of that society from which we have been so fortuitously delivered—they come not only from selfish appetite, but also from power and the many forms of its abuse. Where all is known, and all are equal, and all serve the same unifying purpose, these aberrations cannot exist.'

Moss was silent. 'Can all this be possible?' he wondered. Somewhere in the village a perfumed wood was burning in a hearth, the smoke wreathing across the terrace. Its scent caused him to sigh in sleepy contentment. Nunez watched him attentively as the lines of tension eased from his face.

'I have work that I must do. Sleep now, my son. Recoup your strength. In the evening, at your feast of welcoming, we will talk more together.'

He walked off, and Moss stood up, moved across the terrace, feeling the stones through his pampooties, rejoicing in a new way of walking, an easy transference of weight and balance from foot to foot, a deliberation prefiguring each step, a natural elegance and ease that he remembered from the best times in his climbing. Now it was to be his way of existing in the world, and it carried him up the stairs of the house to his bed, where he fell once more into deep and peaceful sleep.

The season of summer with its soft winds slipped away, in its place along the whole long length of the valley the fire-tints of autumn. Feathered elegance of bare birch branches brushed their delicacy across heavier swathes of colour: the veronese green of October rhododendron, and the lighter tones and texture of juniper, with its piquant blue berries, gritty in the mouth, on which Moss chewed continually as he went about his work. The hillsides were burnished, patched and gilded with red and flame and copper. In forest glades, and across riverside alps, long grasses that rippled in the breeze took on the colour of ripe corn, golden in the morning sunlight. The glacier-melt opacities of the summer torrents had all washed away, a steady flow of pure crystal in their place. Even the air seemed to sparkle, especially in the sharpness of morning frosts, which intensified the season's colours and made the high white mountain peaks above seem so close in the clear air that they could almost be touched.

The whole community of the valley set to harvesting and gathering, the wheat and oats and barley scythed and stooked and brought in to the threshing floors. Cartloads of huge marrows, bright in their yellow and orange; cucumbers and onions and earthy mounds of potatoes; apples and apricots and sour-sweet brilliant kumquats and succulent pears—all carried from the growing terraces and stored in the village barns and root-cellars. The long ravine above its roaring river was searched and illuminated day after day by sunshine, and steeped in gorgeous rich ripeness.

The threshed grains were stored in sacks for grinding, and the village cats patrolled the granaries purposefully and grew sleek and fat. The weavers and tailors were busy preparing thick felted clothes for the coming winter; Moss's pampooties were put aside for heavier boots, fleece-lined and warm. In the long evenings the community met indoors, spinning and weaving by the light of beeswax candles in reflective metal lanterns, making wattle hurdles for lambing-time, and baskets of the long, pliable hazel-wands as singers, musicians and story-tellers performed. The shortening daytime saw the bare land tended after the labour of its fruitfulness. Its terraces were top-dressed with manure. The fruit trees were carefully pruned so that their vigour would be retained and the weight of next year's crops would not damage their branches.

When he was not helping with these tasks and learning the skills necessary for their execution, Moss worked each day in the woods with Nunez. They planted out saplings from the plant-nursery close to the village to replace felled timber, lowering them into holes filled with rich, crumbled leaf-loam and water, spreading out their root-balls gently in the black liquid, back-filling and staking the slender growth. Nunez would spread around each planted tree a handful of seeds and leaves from a sack he carried.

'The deer, the pigs and the bears avoid this plant, though it harms neither the trees nor us. It gives them the chance to grow tall and strong, for otherwise they would be damaged or destroyed. So too our children in this valley...'

Often they would encounter the professor of botany and her daughter, walking with a swift grace and rapt attention through the clearings intent on distant parts of the woods, carrying woven baskets on their backs for the plants they collected. Sometimes, if Moss and Nunez were brewing tea over a small fire as winter came on, and eating their lunch of flat breads and pungent round goat's cheeses rolled in oats and cracked peppercorns, the two women would join them, share food and drink, talk of what birds and animals they had seen in the woods, and depart in a swirl of skirts and womanly elegance. And the woman would steal a quick, sidelong glance at her daughter's face as they walked away, and Nunez would register the thoughtful expression on the face of his adoptive son.

One day, a mile from the village in the forest, Nunez led Moss down a broad path into a grove of tall pine-trees. He pointed up into the branches, where bundles of bamboo secured with cord hung high above the ground.

'This is our sacred grove, the place where our spirits take leave of our bodies, and the latter are given back to the growing world.'

Moss peered up at the bundles, puzzled.

'After death,' Nunez explained, 'the flies, the bees, the birds come and feed on the corpse; maggots consume it away, hatch out into the flies that are eaten by flycatcher, thrush or spider; or they fall to the ground along with the disarticulated bones and are devoured by bears or hogs. This burial of the air is a form of rebirth; but a lowly one from what has been left behind, whilst the spirit continues on its journey. See there!'

Nunez pointed to a bundle clearly more recent than the rest, across which a few birds searched and probed with their long beaks, teasing out fat maggots through the close weave of the bamboo.

'This is the mother of my Dear One and the grandmother of the professor of botany. She died some weeks before you arrived. She had lived a hundred and seventeen summers. Before her passing into the spirit-world, she told her daughter and grand-daughter of your coming. "A man from the fallen world, on his way now, soon you will see him high on Parasco." Do you remember, when you met with the elders in council, the flight of laughing-thrushes? They had come from their feasting here. All knew the sign. It was your acceptance...'

On another day, as he and Nunez were finishing their work, a troupe of children came marching through the glade, singing, baskets of fungi on their arms. Nunez greeted them with a wave and smile and beckoned.

'We are the two men who came from beyond Parasco,' he told them.

'What is that world beyond the mountain like?' asked a slender girl of nine or ten who seemed to be spokesperson of the group. Nunez and Moss looked at each other, and after a thoughtful pause the latter replied:

'Old and hungry as a bear who has lost his teeth. Wicked as the demons who lead you to wrong and thorny paths.'

The children all grimaced, and carried on their way, singing a rhythmical chant in high, piping voices. Moss watched them, an expression of curiosity on his face.

'We do not worship our children here, as they do in the countries we left,' said Nunez. 'Nor do we abuse them. Are not these polarities most telling! We educate them, and open for them the Way and the power of the mind. You may feel that our stress on unity works against individuality, and restricts the growth of the mind. We do not find it to be so. The way in which the society from which you have come so recently was manipulated into believing in, and beyond that worshipping, vague and dangerous concepts like individuality, freedom of expression, choice, has removed from it all discipline, all notion of the development of a craft through rigour, application and long study.'

Moss glimpsed the flash of passion in Nunez's eye, bent his head to listen as he continued:

'It has left that society assailed by the cacophonous baying of the mob. What use the voice of the people when the people have nothing worthy to say? It was through these vices that Franco and the Falangists held on to power in the land of my youth. Here they have no place. Here we are free within the contracts we accept, and safe and happy too.'

Spring came in a torrent of opening buds, violets carpeting the woodland floor, birdsong rising each dawn to deafening pitch at the sun's rising. Moss visited all the other occupations open to him, but it was accepted that he belonged with Nunez in the woods, and he learnt more of the woodland crafts. When the saplings he had replanted showed the red points of budding along their silvery bark, he felt a thrill he could not recall ever having known.

He revelled in the quiet attention and minimal speech of the old man who had become his daily companion, and watched him attentively, studying the economical grace of his movement, the weighing and measuring in contemplation of a task and then the unhurried swift completion. Sometimes, in the lengthening days, Nunez's Dear One would leave her loom and walk up to share their basket of provisions. Moss would observe the ease, the familiarity and clear affection between them, expressed through inflection and the smallest gesture, without any grasping signifiers of possession on either side. It made him at once deeply happy to witness, and at the same time wondering and unresolved. But he knew that he had found his home place in this community, and his vocation in the woodland work. The life of the forest thrilled into him, and a kind of serene acceptance settled into his soul.

One day, when Nunez had walked down to the forge to discuss with the smiths their charcoal requirements for smelting, Moss—after thinning out the underbrush in a copse of birch—was sitting on an anemone-spangled bank of moss, a small stream flowing past and the brightly-coloured robins of the valley chasing around in their mating frenzy. He had water in a pot coming to the boil on a small fire of cleared twigs, and cheese and bread spread out on a cloth when he saw the woman of the forest, his guide's Dear One, approaching by herself from the far side of the clearing. She greeted him with a wave; walked across, stopped close by, slung the basket of plants she carried off her shoulder, hoisted up her skirt, untied the cord of her drawers and squatted to piss.

Moss watched as the clear trickle ran down for two or three feet before being absorbed into the grass. His mind flashed back to a summer evening on the lawn of the walled garden behind the Sheffield flat he had shared with Lynette. There came into his mind the image of himself lying there naked in the warm darkness, street-lamps paling the sky and obliterating the stars, and Lynette giggling as she squatted above him and pissed on his face. He had lain catatonic with shock and affront, as she had laughed at him:

'Golden rain! That's what every man needs—to get pissed on by the women of the world.'

In the same nexus of memories came recollection of her relating how his work-colleague and college friend Roger Allott had told her to do this to him, 'and he wouldn't mind if I did it to him next,' she'd added. And had she obliged, asked Moss? She screwed her face into enigmatic expression, pursed her lips, and left his question hanging in the fraught air between them. He slipped with a shudder away from the memory as he had slipped damply from under Lynette that night, glanced across to where the woman of the forest had plucked a pad of dry moss from the bank and was blotting herself between the thighs, stooping afterwards to press it back into the place from which it came.

'We use this moss for so many things,' she smiled at him, 'your head, remember?' and she re-arranged herself as he watched without the least embarrassment on either side. He made a tea with forest herbs she passed across to him from her basket. They drank, ate the provisions laid out. She moved close behind him, parted his hair and examined the scar of the wound she had stitched months before, taking a small phial of oil from a pocket in her skirt and rubbing it tenderly into his scalp.

'My daughter has asked me to speak to you.'

She spoke in a low, serious voice close to his ear, re-corked the phial of oil and put it away.

'She has watched you through the autumn and winter, has attuned to the music of your speech, has asked about you of your work-companion, the man you now accept as your father. When first she tended you in your sickness, though you are not strong as our men are, she felt the stirrings of attraction in her breasts and her loins. I have watched her through this time, and as a mother have known. I have watched you too for signs of the corruption that exists in that world from which you came. I am happy with her choice. Now she has come to her decision. She desires to breed by you, and for you to be her Dear One. Will you take her as your Dear One, man from afar?'

Moss met the unwavering gaze of the woman of the forest.

'You know already the answer that is in my heart. Must I form my lips around it for custom's sake?'

'Yes.'

'Then yes. Already she is the Dear One of my every thought.'

'You know the way of our community. You know our practice. Only when you move beyond desire do you perceive the object in all its splendour. Only then do you begin to love. We have all made the sacrifice to gain the pure happiness. Do you have the strength?'

'I would die for shame if I were found wanting.'

'I will go to my daughter, and tell her, that she may be glad.'

The woman of the forest shouldered her basket, made the flowing gesture from forehead to lips to breast, and as gently as she had arrived she departed across the soft turf so brightly braided with eyebright, fenugreek and veronica, leaving Moss to reflect on his own swelling happiness.

Nunez returned to find Moss swinging the heavy bill-hook among the crowded scrub of the birch-copse, letting more and more light in among the pale trees, singing to himself as he dragged out faggots bound with woodbine and hangman's garland.

'So, my son, the woman of the forest has brought you to the place of understanding. I am glad her daughter has made you her choice.'

He drew Moss to him in close embrace, helped him drag out the last of the trimmings, and together they walked down through the trees to the village as the sun rolled down to the bounding ridge. Skeins of wild geese on their spring migration from the valleys of their wintering to the high plains beyond the mountains flew high overhead, their calls echoing down. Villagers on their terraces looked up and watched as they wavered past. They sensed their own being harmonizing with the great movements of nature. Shadow welled up from the depths of the valley, bringing night's peace. The fires were lit in the village hearths. Sweet smoke rose from the chimneys in the still air and mingled

82

in a blue haze over the houses that slowly drifted away into the trees. Nunez turned down the path to his dwelling, and Moss climbed up to the terrace where the woman of the forest and his guide awaited him, sitting at the table with their daughter, who greeted him with sparkling eyes and a bursting grin. And he held her gaze and smiled, knowing how economical, and how much more expressive therefore, were the community's signs of affection.

That night Nunez and his Dear One joined them for food at the table on the terrace. The young ones were seated together, garlands of spring flowers around their necks. The young men of the kitchen brought plates of chappatis, dishes of dhal bright with turmeric and red chillies, bowls of rice and potato reeking of methi, garlic and asa foetida, little ramekins of okra in rich brown onion sauce, trays of aloo paratha that were charred and running with ghee, jugs of lassi sweetened with honey.

After all had eaten their fill and the dishes on the table had been cleared away, the woman of the forest stood behind her daughter's seat, and Nunez's Dear One behind that of Moss. The young woman, knowing what to do, stood and turned to her mother. Moss followed suit, facing his attendant. Around the wrists of both, the older women placed woven bracelets of bright vermilion threads, knotting them tightly. Then all four were seated again.

The guide, who had watched the women perform this ceremony in which not a word had been uttered, then spoke.

'These are the red threads that bind a man and a woman together in fated and enduring union. Imperishable, unfading, and never to be removed…'

He pushed up the sleeve of his tunic, looked at the bracelet on his wrist, that was still as bright as the evening it had first been fastened there twenty-two years before, and turned his gaze briefly on the woman of the forest, who lifted her sleeve to reveal the bracelet on her own wrist.

Nunez and his Dear One also took up the moment of display as the guide continued.

'...they express the vows on which our unions are founded, the blood that flows on parturition, the sadness of separation that is the risk lovers must face, and the life-giving joy. May your souls in the flight that is life be free as birds through this union. Our elders have carefully studied the auguries for this. They give their consent and are glad. Now is the time of your transformations, when you connect with the spiritual energies of our people. Ignorance and grasping is boundless in the world beyond our confines. We have vowed through our customs and disciplines to keep the example that may transform and uproot it all, to do so here in quiet attendance until all beings are liberated. You join us now whole and united in the perpetuation of this task.

'Tomorrow we escort you to the Hidden Temple for the ceremony of blessing. There you will remain, alone together in the rest house. May your journey be joyful and your union one of harmony and understanding. Of your child's destiny, it is already foretold, and most favourably. Let us rest now, and prepare ourselves through contemplation for these holy things.'

A light brush of her fingers against Moss's wrist and his betrothed stepped away. The guide's powerful hand rested on his shoulder. Nunez came to sit on his other side. Tea was brought to them, poured sweet and frothing from a tall and burnished pot. The guide, in soft tones, spoke again.

'It is hard to renounce that which we so briefly enjoy. Yet to wish otherwise is to rail against our destiny, which is an impiety against nature. In our community, we accept the symbol that expresses our mortal condition, our transience. Life is no more than a sequence of moments distilled out from eternity. Who can remember or recount even forty such? Therefore, despite their scarcity, let them be incandescent in their beauty, eternal in the mind, and above all, blessed by our gratitude.'

The summits of Parasco shone at the valley-head next morning as the party wound its way along the path out of the village—ten people in all, led by the tall old man who had addressed Moss at the council meeting of his welcoming. Her parents and Moss's proxy parents; the young men of the kitchen who would themselves one day follow this path; the two young people entering the state of union: each of them was laden down with heavy baskets of provisions. They toiled in the sunshine up the steep zig-zags that led round a forested spur and dropped down into a concealed valley of high pastures where the Hidden Temple was to be found. A simple log-built rest-house stood alongside, and a stone tank with steps leading down into it, filled by a stream issuing from hot mineral springs above. Beyond the temple a fierce torrent cascaded out of a ravine into a long pool of clear green water, and was stilled.

Their burdens were placed within the rest-house, and the woman of the forest and the young men of the kitchen set to work. A table and chairs were brought out on to the verandah and the rooms swept. The woman of the forest and the Dear One of Nunez made up a bed with sheets of fine lawn from their baskets, spread on it a duck-down quilt, cambric-covered, and put soft pillows of feather and Indian cotton at its head. They strewed petals from the early dog-roses that were newly in bloom across the bed, met each other's eyes across it and smiled in gentle remembrance; then they directed the young men to work at preparing food as they walked across the few yards to the temple.

Their eyes adjusted to the gloom inside. They saw the tall old man, candles burning on the altar-table behind him, on the wall above it a silk hanging, vividly embroidered. It depicted a chasm of immense depth, a torrent gushing down, the walls lipping over so that they were no more

85

than ten yards apart at their top. A powerful figure was suspended forever mid-leap, halfway across, a long procession of figures waiting their turn behind him.

In the reality of the Hidden Temple the two young people knelt at the feet of the old priest. The woman of the forest walked in to stand at her daughter's side. Nunez was by that of Moss. He nudged him gently, gestured to the hanging.

'This is called The Leap of Faith. It shows how our community first came here, before the Spirit Bridge was built.'

The priest held up a finger to silence him, and began to speak.

'You make today this singular and binding contract, for the preservation of our unity and for your own future happiness. The spirits have been watching over you, have brought you to this point. Observe the conditions of the discipline you enter, and joy is yours, futurity for our community assured. I call down the blessing of the spirits upon you.'

A bell rang. The couple turned their faces up towards him, he touched their foreheads with vermilion dye, and they bowed their heads. He held out his hands in blessing above them. In a flurry of wings a tiny bird, its underparts pale, a brilliant yellow crest along its crown, alighted on his wrist, claws clinging to his bracelet of union, and began to sing a sequence of short wheezing notes.

For the first time, our lovers clasped hands as all present watched the manifestation on the priest's wrist. He raised his hand, opened the palm in gesture of farewell, and the bird flew out of the temple and back into the forest from which it had come. The lovers embraced, and their attendants led them out and across to the guest-house stilled and joyful at the apparition they had seen.

On the guest-house verandah food was ready. They sat around the table. No-one mentioned the tiny bird, as though to have talked of it would have revoked its uncanny blessing. Only the woman of the forest spoke.

'My daughter, my new son—know that there is goodness and magic in the world—know that your union is the conduit for its expression. Obey the customs of our community, whatever the apparent cost. Your blessings are attendant on that discipline, our unity dependent upon it. In fourteen days, before the time of woman is due upon you, daughter, return together to the village. Fourteen more days and you may come here again. For my Dear One, your father, and me this process took several moons. Do not be anxious. Take pleasure in each other, and come to know. And so will the pattern be, until you are with child. Our house will then be home to you and your Dear One so long as you both shall live.'

She embraced her daughter, and Moss too, and side by side with the guide, along with the old priest, she and the others departed by the village path that led round the ridge and down past the threshing-floors and the granaries into the long street where the men and women, proud of the sweetness that was in their lives, went humbly about their ordinary tasks.

And so the two young people, who until that point had scarcely exchanged meaningful words—though many had been the looks that had passed between them—were left alone in the high green cwm, with the pattern of their future life set out before them. The young women of the forest took the initiative, leading Moss—who was bashful and shy despite his sexual experience in the other life—across by the hand to the bathing-place of the hot springs.

'Come,' she said, disrobing on the bank, 'to teach you I am naked first.'

And she walked from him and descended the stone steps into the tank, and he undressed and followed her, laughing as the clean, clear water rose up his legs, plunging into it and surfacing by her side, and she turned to him, they clasped one another close, she clung to him, wrapped her legs around his waist, his arms supporting her as he entered her gently; she sighed at his ear as her hymen was ruptured, wincing, soothed by the mineral warmth of the water, relaxing into the gentle rocking rhythm between them that quickened until the climactic moment in which all tension was released in the deepest sigh, and he was held in her firm and liquid grasp until her thighs relaxed and she slipped down to kiss him passionately once again.

They walked entranced and naked, carrying their clothes, across to the rest-house and the bed and there made love again and again, lingeringly, she teaching him to control himself and delay, imparting to him the secrets her mother had whispered to her over the last days, and that she had had from her mother and her from hers back through generations and centuries.

In morning sunlight on the verandah, dreamy from their love-making, he quizzed how she, a virgin, had come by such erotic knowledge?

'It is our women's lore,' she teased, 'and through it our Dear Ones are at our command. But this sweet time until I am with child is all we have. It can never become a mechanical compulsion, as with those from the outer world. Henceforwards it lives in our memories alone; and it is told that I shall have no daughter to whom the secrets of my lineage can be passed on. And nor will our son, as Rinpoche, have a Dear One of his own.'

'May we not leave together? Live as one forever? Have many children and a life outside the valley?'

'What? Would you have me prepare the juice of the aconite, that banishes all memories, robs us of their precious store, and take me sojourning empty-handed into barren lands where there is no unity or rest? And to do that for a bloom that fades, when we may grow together in beauty and live well? The sacrifice we have agreed brings with it all that is good. Store now in the granary of your heart these present memories that will ever sustain you. Come back now to the threshing-floor of our bed and let us lay in more…'

Again she was naked before him. He watched the curve of her back with the red-gold of her hair hanging down, the smooth swell of her movement towards the bed, the jut of her breasts and firmness of her nipples as she turned to him, legs parted to reveal the mossy thicket of hair between her thighs into which, having bounded across, he buried his face and sucked and licked until she clung to him, bucked against him in rising ecstasy, and shuddered to her climax, from which she relaxed to pull his face up to hers, take him inside her once again, and let the rhythm between them build once more.

So the days passed. In due course they descended to the village. For two more cycles they returned to the Hidden Temple and the rest-house, to the hot springs in the high green cwm, and experienced the joy of knowing each other.

One morning, towards the end of her third cycle since their blessing, she woke with a metallic taste in her mouth, her breasts tender and nausea passing over her in waves. She turned to Moss, who was stirring from sleep by her side, and spoke to him.

'My Dear One, I am with child. Hold me now. Our time of physical union is at an end. Our transformation has begun. In two days we will return to the village. In nine months our son will be born, who will become Rinpoche at Kartaphu in his time.'

Moss opened his eyes on a vision of loveliness and loss, through which the unbearable beauty of the world was accepted into his soul and he became one.

'Yes, my Dear One,' he smiled. 'I am so very glad…'

And he held her very near and circled round her with reverence and solicitude for the remnants of their time in that high and holy place. The red squirrels chased down out of the tall pines and played across their verandah, jumping on to the table and making off with pieces of sweet naan that she held out to them. Their little, chiselled faces watched her attentively, tufted ears twitching, tails a-thrash, measuring the wisdom of trust; then they darted in and raced away harum scarum to the pines, where they chittered in animation at their action and its reward. Goldcrests sang in the eaves and flurried down for crumbs. And the Dear Ones smiled and leant close, and held each other through their last nights together, but already their physical love-making was a thing of the past, the child growing in her body their precious focus now. On a morning of crystal brilliance they shut the door of the rest-house for the last time and walked across to the deodars on the bounding ridge, sat there under the drooping branches on the scented earth, and she laid her head in his lap and took his hand in hers.

'My Dear One', she said, 'though this time has passed, my heart holds its every memory clear as air. My heart is yours. And our child will spread goodness in the world. I am so glad you came over Parasco and into our valley. We will maintain this dear and peaceful place.'

They walked slowly down into their village, and their steps were firm and resolute, though they echoed plaintively into the valley they had left behind.

The woman in the front seat of the Land Cruiser tilted the mirror towards her, ran the coral lipstick around her chapped mouth and fluffed up the hair her hat had flattened, flicking aside the strands from her temples and carefully replacing her sunglasses on top of her head. The driver observed her in the corner of his eye.

'Here we go, Lyn—Kartaphu!'

He pointed to the huddle of shacks by the tarmac, the towering monastery dwarfing them. She pursed her lips and reached across to rub the inside of his thigh—a woman in her sixties, exquisitely groomed and preserved. She glanced round to observe the rest of the Land Cruiser's complement. Their hands were pressed together as they started to chant. She quickly reclaimed her hand and followed suit. The vehicle left the tarmac, drew up by the *dhaba* in a swirl of cold dust, and the people eased themselves out, apart from the refined woman, whose mobile gave its 'text received' tone. She held it up to read the message.

'Daddy says to tell I wrote off yr R/Rover on lane down to Hpierpoint. Is v. cross about NCB. New one here by time you back. Am going up to town to stay in flat for while till he's calmed down. Love u mama. Mwah mwah.'

'Fucking Timmy!' she snapped, pocketed the phone and climbed out to join the others.

'So do we get to be received by the new Rinpoche?'

'Maybe tomorrow,' replied the sleek Canadian guide, pushing aside glossy curls the wind had blown into his eyes.

'And do we stay here?'

'There should be rooms for us in the rest-house.'

'Doubles?'

'I'll see what I can do,' he responded, a hint of weariness in his voice, 'but listen, Lyn, we're not supposed to—you know… Not within the monastery.'

'Fuck that!' she snapped. 'Who's to tell us what we can and can't do in the privacy of our own room?'

She strode off towards the *dhaba*, a commanding woman in her early sixties, fit, well-groomed, supple of body, remarkably handsome, her unbuttoned top flaunting an impressive cleavage,

'Chai!' she said to the proprietor, 'Two. And two Maza as well.'

She sat down on the bench. The Canadian tour-guide was talking to a heavy woman from Barnes with damp patches of perspiration under her arms.

'Wade—I'm over here. I've ordered chai,' the first woman shouted across, and then scanned round. Across the tarmac a man sat with his back to a wall, tanned, in the local dress, wearing pampooties and a conical head-dress. She studied him. There was something familiar about his features, his self-containment. He met her gaze, and looked away, reading instead the lettering on the Toyota's side.

'*Circle of Western Buddhists, Richmond and Barnes chapter, Kathmandu-Kathgodam-Kailash Pilgrimage 2039.*'

She noticed the ornate bronze bowls, three-legged and with strange ear-shaped handles on either side, that were strapped on to his pack. She walked across.

'Are these for sale?' she asked, puzzled at how she might know him. He shook his head and slipped her gaze once more, knowing the uselessness of explaining their purpose to her. His mind was on the return journey that he had made many times after trading here. He thought of the crossing of the Spirit Bridge, thought that even after forty years of knowledge since the first time he'd crossed the beauty and wonder of it still held him in awe.

'How did they ever get that keystone in place,' he reflected, 'above a two-thousand-foot drop? Just walking over it, just looking down into that river—even now it leaves my senses reeling. And as for jumping across…'

He was remembering the story Nunez had told him—of how, chased out of the land beyond the Seven Valleys, the people had first come to the fortunate place; how they had leapt across the gap, taken the Leap of Faith. He drifted away into wonderment.

A voice snagged against his reflections.

'If you won't sell me the brass pots, do you mind this…' it asked, the speaker pointing the camera on her mobile at him. He held up his hand in a gesture of refusal, dismissal. She swung round and walked away impatiently.

'Fucking precious natives,' she muttered under her breath, and ran into the heavy woman, who had drifted across towards her.

'Margaret, did Wade say what time we'd be meeting to chant?'

They walked back to the bench by the *dhaba*, and joined Wade. 'Oh Margaret, will you have some *chai*?' he asked, and strode off to fetch another cup.

As he stood waiting, he noticed the red-haired woman come out of the monastery and walk across to the man by the wall. They shouldered their burdens, and headed off along a well-trodden path that led into the hills.

'Who are those guys, Lobsang?' Wade enquired of the ancient man who was preparing the chai.

'Their son is the new Rinpoche. They have been visiting him. He has given them bronze ritual bowls he had cast for the Hidden Temple, that show which spirits are beneficent, which noxious, and tell of what opens the Way and what closes it. They are not for your people. No-one can buy them. Their powers are dangerous to those who do not understand their use. These people are of the tribe from beyond the Seven Valleys, across the Spirit Bridge.'

'A long trek?'

'Many days. Very difficult. No-one go there but these people. Yetis and demons...'

'Sure, plenty of those,' Wade replied, curiosity satisfied, and ambled back, dribbling *chai* as he went, to re-join his clients and tell them when they might chant.

Incident at Mew Stone Point

a rock-climbing romance

In a little hollow where the rougher grasses grew longer, a blue butterfly fluttered and could not get out. He was entangled with his own wings, he could not guide himself between the grass tops; his wings fluttered and carried him back again. The grass was like a net to him, and there he fluttered till the wind lifted him out, and gave him the freedom of the hills.
Richard Jefferies, 'Clematis Lane'

It was one of those warm evenings of early April. Easter was late that year. The clocks had gone forward, but it was approaching dusk as I walked up Highgate Hill. A group of us used to meet every Wednesday in The Crown, to arrange transport for the weekend climbing trips. I ducked into the pub doorway and ran into Nicky, who was just on his way out, hand in hand with a young woman I'd seen him with from a distance around town a time or two over the last few weeks.

'Hi Bob,' he said, a sheepish look on his face, 'Are we still on for Pembroke this Friday?'

'Sure,' I said, and was going to suggest when and where I'd pick him up when his companion spoke up.

'We're just going for a look at Karl Marx's tomb—workers of the world unite, and all that, though maybe not in the way he meant! Sorry we can't stop.'

'Oh, this is Fran. I don't think you've met? Fran—Bob—he teaches in our old place. Been there throughout eternity. Look, we're going to hop over the gate into the cemetery for a walk round.'

He blushed as he said it. She winked at me.

'We'll be back in ten…'

'It'd better take longer than that, buddy,' she butted in, 'or I'll tell everyone we know and that'll ruin your chances as the gay Lothario about town for ever and a day.'

Nicky looked abashed. 'Less of the *gay* Lothario, if you please—that's no way for a women's-libber to talk. Sympathy for your fellow-oppressed!' he pouted.

'Women's Lib? That's so last year. Post-liberation party-season now, mate. Good-time girls on top! Here, Bob was it… Hold my bag and don't run away. We'll be back in thirty or thereabouts…'

She swung a heavy old tapestry thing she was wearing across her shoulder at me, and with an impudent grin and a roll of her eyes, she tugged him away and they ran across the road. I watched them go, amused and rather touched by them—him. Contained and calculating behind the relaxed and boyish demeanour, slim, almost frail, with a mane of fair hair hanging over his shoulders; her, so brave and riding for a fall, sturdier, dark curls framing a pert, pretty face and animated features that danced with good humour. Her white knickers flashed in the gloaming from under her short skirt as she climbed the gate, swung her legs over and dropped down the other side to wrestle with Nicky as he tried to catch her. She saw me still looking and waved for me to join them. I held up a hand in gesture of surrender, and disappeared inside the pub.

All the usual boys were there—J.K., Kenny, Baz, Dave, both Als, The Conman, Irish Mick, Taxi Driver and a few others, standing around in a circle guffawing and slopping their pints as each tried to outdo everyone else with *bons mots* and one-liners polished all week in the dreary work-hours and now belted out without any need to listen to anyone else's. I bought a pint of Young's and went to sit at a window table to distance myself from the racket and the beer-mist they were gusting around, tossing Fran's bag on the bench seat and easing myself in after it.

'They look like a pack of baboons, don't they—red-nosed instead of red-arsed, seeing who can howl loudest and whose jaws gape widest. Think they'll end up swallowing each other…'

I turned to register the woman on the next table who'd spoken. She was still studying the men in front of the bar, an expression on her face of benign contempt. I put her at about my age. Wavey dark hair and brown eyes with laughter-lines at the corners. There was a pint of Guinness on the table in front of her, almost finished, and a Francois Mauriac novel in one of those thick, uncut editions. I remember it as *Therese Desqueyroux*, but she swears it was *Le Noeud de Viperes*.

'Mind you,' she continued after a pause, 'get a gang of girls together and they can ratchet up the decibels. But somehow they don't look as helpless. Crazy maybe, but this lot are such a bunch of buffoons. How d'you take them seriously?'

'Maybe I don't,' I responded, 'Why would you? But you know—they're good enough company, providing you've got an interest in common.'

'I have that, but I think I'd need a bit more to be involved in that group. So you're one of the climbers, are you?'

She studied me, head on one side at the approved coquette angle, eyes sparkling with fun, and gravity too.

'You don't quite look the type. And you're not loud enough. Are you off to Bosherston this weekend?'

Nicky and Fran arrived back before I could fumble for a response. Fran hurled herself on to the bench seat alongside me.

'Want a drink, you two?' I asked.

'Lager shandy for me, and Nicky needs a large whisky. I don't think Karl would've approved. He liked to expatiate with force and at length. All that dogmatic disquisition, and what it comes down to is a cold tombstone against a bare arse—against his bare arse I hasten to add. Girls on top tonight. Followed by oysters, wasn't it Nicky?'

I glanced an apologetic enquiry at the woman on the next table and she made a brief, elegant gesture of refusal, a hand over her glass, turning away with a hovering smile. When I came back with the drinks she was gone.

'Well that wasn't the worst I've ever had,' Fran began, 'and it wasn't the shortest either. And it was in the weirdest place. Reasons to be cheerful, I suppose. Anyway, I made him perform the appropriate penance for being over-hasty so I'm happy enough. Sticky knickers, though. However, I come well equipped with a spare pair—what every wanton needs! Where's my bag, Bob?'

I handed it across, she delved in and produced a pair with bright polka dots, which she proceeded to wave about. Nicky looked heavenwards.

'Fran, you're as bad as a man,' he sighed.

'You should see my used-tampons lampshade,' she laughed, in response to his embarrassed expression, 'I'm going to enter it for the Turner Prize. Just got to work on the two-thousand-word conceptual appreciation to go with —want to help me, Mr. Philosopher?'

The men in front of the bar, picking up on the drift of the conversation, were casting curious looks over in our direction.

'Come on, Nicky, make your arrangements—'something for the weekend, sir?'—so we can go back to mine. I don't mind the odd *al fresco*, but the workers need to take time over their uniting. I've got a nice bottle of *Pinot Grigio* chilling in the fridge that I'll entertain myself with if you're not up to it again tonight. Nice to meet you, Bob. When I've worn him out, I might give you a seven-days-free-trial.'

Nicky blushed and snorted into his beer, Fran disappeared off to the loo, and we arranged to meet on Friday.

'I can finish in Holborn by two—how about you pick me up at three outside Turnham Green tube, then we're straight on the M4? I'll take my gear for the weekend in to work, I can get the District line down there and we'll be well away before the holiday hordes.'

I'd just moved in to a big, light garden flat on Abinger Road so that suited me fine.

'You're on. Are you bringing a tent, or shall I?'

'I'll bring one from the shop, and if either of us gets lucky, the other's sleeping on the beach—or in the car if it's pissing down.'

'Shouldn't be—forecast's good. The odd shower late on Saturday, it said.'

He worked in *Alpine Adventures* and could help himself to whatever he needed.

'Bring a couple of long ropes', I prompted. 'I've something in mind. As to the tent arrangements, chance'd be a fine thing.'

'You looked to be doing alright when we came in just then.'

'Oh, with her?' I gestured at the empty place. 'Never seen her before, and I don't suppose I will again.'

'What about all those gorgeous students in your department?'

'You don't go there—*in statu pupillaris* and all that. Instant dismissal on grounds of gross moral turpitude, and quite right too.'

'You mean even if one comes on strong, you wouldn't?'

'Nope—not the done thing. And apart from that, it's big trouble if you're found out, quite apart from all the power-imbalance. Definitely abusive stuff if you see it from that perspective.'

'Think I'll stick with the retail trade, then. Academia sounds a bit too dry and regulated for me. Anyway, a post as shop assistant is what a first in philosophy gets you these days. You were on the last lifeboat when Maggie torpedoed *H.M.S. Tenure*, lost with all hands…'

I was going to deconstruct his metaphor, point out the contradictions and risk his habitual accusation of pedantry when Fran re-appeared, looped her arms around him and bent down to bite his ear.

'That's right, Nicky darling. We don't want dry. Come on now—are you ready again yet? We workers have things to do.'

'Unhand me, harlot,' he mouthed, squirming out of her grasp, and to me he said 'OK Turnham Green, Friday at three. See you there *avec* tent,' and with that the pair of them sashayed out of the door, all eyes above the guffawing mouths before the bar swivelling towards them, then dropping to focus on her round behind in the tight skirt as she disappeared outside.

'So who's Fran, then, Nicky?' I asked, once we were free of the Heathrow and M25 traffic and stepping westwards at the usual mad pace on Friday afternoon.

'She was a mate of Kate's.'

'Was…'

'Definitely past tense. Kate had warned her about me after that business at her parents' over Christmas.'

'What, when she walked in on you snogging her sister?'

'Well, it was a bit more than snogging actually. How would The Crook describe it? "Just getting the top R.P.'s in, mate!"'

He imitated the high lisping Scouse accent of a regular climbing friend of ours, and carried on with his story: 'Anyway, Kate duffed me out over that, horrid scenes, tears, separate beds, her dad driving me to Oxted station on Boxing Day in icy silence. She told Fran what a bastard I am, and psychology worked its usual weird and wonderful magic. They're in the same chambers together. Also, Fran was looking for a bit of week-time diversion. She's hooked up with some guy in Norwich, heads back there every weekend or he comes down here—good job, good prospects, nice flat, spoils her rotten and wants to marry her. So she's having a bit of fun before she settles down. It's like that situation you were in before Maddy, isn't it? Tell us that story again. I'm still not sure if I believe you, or if you're just pulling my pisser.'

'What, the one about Chrissie, and how Maddy and I got together?'

'Yeah, that one—I call it the tale of the witch of Muswell Hill—I've told it around all over the place. Told 'em you swear it's true.'

'It is true. You heard it from Maddy as well, remember.'

'I heard a version of it from Maddy. D'you still miss her? Long time to be in mourning. It's been, what, more than ten years now. You over it yet? Or 'found closure' as they say…'

'No, not yet. Doubt I ever will be. Not easy watching the woman you love die, and of cancer especially…'

'I guess not. Though assuming what you tell me's true, ten years is a long time to go without a fuck, especially at your age. It might drop off, you know, and I read in *The Guardian* that abstinence definitely increases the odds on getting prostate trouble in your seventies—should you get that far, and the way you climb I have my doubts. Anyway, come on—no moping. We've climbs to do this weekend, and I've a feeling one of them is going to be mega! I brought the long ropes, incidentally. Now how does the story begin?'

We were already out beyond Reading, and the traffic was thinning out.

'It was in my second year at college—yes, I know, the one I'm still teaching at now and have been since years before you arrived. You don't need to remind me how pathetic is that! There was a girl in my tutorial group that

100

year and you know the way things go. You exchange glances, they click somehow, curiosity's aroused. You start sitting next to each other, discussing the work, the lecturers, going for cups of coffee, meeting by chance in the library and working on essays together. Maybe you ask her out to the pictures and end up kissing on her doorstep when you've walked her home. She was called Chrissie—I just told you that, didn't I?'

'No matter—I just accept you're a dementing old git, remember.'

'So, Chrissie—she was a feisty little woman, and I mean little—she was about four feet ten, gave me a crick in the neck bending down to kiss her. She came from Bury St. Edmunds, her dad was a Methodist minister. The fly in the ointment was that she had a bloke back in B.S.E., name of Bernard, worked at a printing firm there and they'd been going out together since they were kids—met at her old man's chapel. She was going to be a teacher. Plan was for her to finish her degree, return to Bury and marry him, then they'd replenish the class numbers, she'd take the Sunday School and he'd print all the textbooks and hymn sheets—you know the sketch…'

'So were you actually fucking each other, or had this guy activated her conscience?'

'Let's say she put the latter in abeyance for a time. How does Burns put it—'Two things without conscience—a wet cunt and a standing prick'? Problem was there were a few incidents. She'd head off to Bury on Fridays and catch the early train on Mondays in time for college. I'd be away climbing every weekend, so I was cool about it and wasn't going to make waves. Best not to do jealousy in any situation. I think her guy got a bit suspicious, though— maybe she'd learned a few tricks she didn't know before, or maybe she dropped a few hints to keep him keen and attentive. There were three or four occasions when he drove down from Bury and turned up at her flat very late.

The bell would ring, she'd peer down and see his car there and I'd be bundled out on to the fire escape in the dark with my clothes and shoes and the curtains drawn behind me while she went down to answer the door. After another occasion when someone downstairs had let him in and he was actually knocking at the door of her flat—he didn't have a key, fortunately—it just got too tense. That's when I went along to see Maddy.'

'Did you know her already, then?'

'Oh yes—she was the aunt of the girl I went out with when I was in my teens—her mother's much younger sister. I met her a few times when her niece and I were still at school, family parties and stuff, and we always got on well. Miranda took a year out to do V.S.O. before uni—they sent her to St. Helena of all places, which wasn't somewhere I could visit even if she'd wanted me to—so she and I did the decent thing and split up to give each other the freedom. Then when I went up to Birkbeck and was living in that subterranean flat on Merriman Road—you know, you arrived there somehow one morning deaf and doped up to the eyeballs, whingeing about tinnitus, after The Who gig in The Valley—I'd go up to Muswell Hill from time to time to see Maddy. She was maybe ten years older than me, so it just felt like an elder sister thing at first, hanging out together, going to see a film at the Finchley Rex now and again, an occasional cup of coffee at hers. She lived by herself in one of those 1920s semis on the way up to Ally Pally. I stayed once after one of The Dead's all-nighters, me tripping, out of it after hanging off the scaffolding for eight hours or however long they played. Forever is how it seemed after what I'd taken. There was one version of 'Uncle John's Band' lasted over an hour. I had a continual feeling that Maddy knew exactly what was going on in my head. But you know, sleeping bag on the sofa, cups of tea, all quite innocent… '

'Until…'

'Well, until the day after Bernard had actually knocked on the door whilst we were *in flagrante*. Coitus interruptus didn't come into it. I was bundled out on to that fire escape bollock-naked and my clothes hurled after me faster than you went over the gate into Highgate cemetery the other night. And the next day at college I got the real cold shoulder, briefest of conversations to tell me that Bernard was driving down again that night and to keep clear. So feeling a bit miffed, come tea-time I trooped off up to Maddy's—she was making her way as one of the young novelists of the time and was reliably at home so long as you respected her work hours—to have a moan about the situation.'

'And did you get a sympathetic hearing?'

'Stranger than that. She heard me out, bit of a wry grin on her face, and then asked if I wanted to do anything about it.'

'Like what?' I asked.

'Next time you know he's coming, we can stop him—if you want, and as long as you're prepared to take the consequences.'

'You remember what she was like—the tousled blonde hair, *gamine* style, huge blue eyes—well she fixed them on me with this look of serious challenge, and gave it me straight:

'The next time you know that Bernard's driving down to London…'

'That's tonight, about now, when he's finished work…'

'So d'you want to stop him?'

'I just laughed. She used to tease me all the time when I was with Miranda. I thought it was another of those wind-ups—except she was keeping a very straight face, not a hint of a joke. And I was intrigued. I wanted to know what she had in mind.

'"Yes, of course I do."

'"Come on then, and you have to do exactly as I tell you —this is dangerous, not kid's stuff like your climbing…"

'She stood up and gestured me to follow. We walked down the passage that led from her sitting room at the front of the house towards the kitchen at the back, and she opened the door to a room I'd never noticed before. We went in. A dark blind was pulled down over the window; a pentagram within a circle had been painted in red on the wooden floor; the walls were covered in arcane symbols— moons and goddesses, vulvas and phalluses, strange combinations of numbers and the like. She lit candles.

'"Take your clothes off and stand in the circle just here," she said. "I'm going to fetch a couple of things we need."

'Two minutes later she was back, and I was still standing there, feeling a tad embarrassed. She was my ex-girlfriend's aunt, for heaven's sake…'

'She was totally fuckable as I recall…'

'Yeah, well—that's you, Nicky, and we know about you. It had never crossed my mind.'

'Really? So what did you do?'

'Just what she told me. She came back in, shot me a quick exasperated look, said "Come on!" and was out of her kit in no time so I had to follow suit and try not to look too obviously in her direction.'

'And then?'

'We squatted in the circle, she put the road atlas and box of pins she'd brought in with her down, opened up the atlas at the Bury page…'

'Remind me where Bury is?'

'Middle of nowhere, halfway between Cambridge and Ipswich—not a place anyone in their right mind would want to go.'

'What did Maddy do next?'

'She worked out all the possible routes Bernard might take—basically it was the A14 across to the A11 down to London—and stuck pins in them. Then she turned to me

—very distracting—she had gorgeous tits, I couldn't help noticing—and told me to put everything else out of my mind and just concentrate on stopping him. I wasn't to wish him any harm, I was just to try and stop him.'

'And…'

'We both squatted there for maybe five minutes, really beamed in, and then she took the pins out, closed the atlas, stood up—this lovely little blonde bush at eye-level that I had a huge urge to wrap my lips around—and said, "OK—that does it." We got dressed, had a cup of tea together, and then I trailed off back down to Greenwich.'

'So did the spell work?'

'Miranda had warned me about her aunt. "You wanna watch yourself around that one," she'd said, "She's well strange!" Anyway, I thought no more about it, went off to The Peak climbing that weekend, was back in college on Monday hoping to see Chrissie and she wasn't around. Didn't see her all week. Called round at her flat a time or two but no sign. Next weekend I was in Wales, didn't get back till very late on Sunday—that was the weekend Kingston and I did *Dinosaur* and *The Skull*, big breakthroughs for me—and she still wasn't in college that Monday, so I called round at hers on the way back to mine that evening, just on the off chance, and she answered the door.'

'What did she tell you?'

'She didn't let me in. She just stood there looking at me, and then she said, "I can't see you again, Bob." I asked her why, feeling a bit querulous, and she said Bernard had been driving down to see her after work the Thursday before last, had been very tired because of the night before, and he'd fallen asleep at the wheel of his car. It was one of those old side-valve, three-gear Ford Pops in beige. I remember hearing it trundle up the street to hers with the gears clicking on one of the nights we were disturbed, seeing it parked outside when I crept down off the fire escape. He'd driven it into a ditch.'

'Was he O.K?'

'Car was a write-off. Another driver saw what happened, he was dragged out and taken to hospital in Ipswich. They kept him in over the weekend for observation because he had concussion. His mother phoned Chrissie and she went straight down there to be with him. "I realized, sitting by his bed, that I truly loved him, and what I've been doing with you has been terrible," she told me, and with that she shut the door. Shut it for good.'

'And you?'

'There was no arguing the point. I could see that. I went straight round to Maddy's, more or less said to her "now look what you've done—Miranda warned me about you!" and she laughed, invited me in, and asked what did I expect and didn't I know about karma? And then she said we can do something about this if you like. I was well wary by this time, pretty shaken, but somehow she fascinated me.'

'I bet I can guess what she did about it.'

'I bet you can—you've got that sixth sense around women, and much good it does you! She said "Come with me," I followed her upstairs, we went in her bedroom, she pushed me down on the bed, we were out of our clothes and into it in seconds and as I recall very seldom emerged from it for the next six months. And I recall too that I didn't dare put a foot wrong the whole time we were together. Wouldn't have done for you, mate. But we had a fantastically good time. I more or less gave up the climbing, did all sorts I'd never have done without her—trips to Rome and Paris and the like, holidays in Greece—and loved it all. Loved her as well, though at another level I was terrified of her. And she helped me enormously with my degree work—where I am now is mostly down to her. All the material I worked on through my doctorate first came up in long talks with her in holidays we had at her ex's villa on Anafi.'

'Cool! Was he there too?'

'No—he was an agent in London, much older than her, got her started on her writing. He was quite amused by her toy-boy fling as he called it, had us round for dinner in Primrose Hill a time or two, and was happy for us to look after the Greek place for those summers—he didn't go there any more. And we were blissed out—got on so easily and well. She was working on her second novel, I was getting an immense amount of reading done for college and talking about it with her when we weren't swimming or taking long siestas or generally shambling around in a loved-up post-coital haze. Very hot island!'

'And then she got ill and was diagnosed?'

'Yes. After we came back from the second summer at Anthony's villa. Ovarian cancer, too advanced for treatment. She was dead in three months from diagnosis. Very calm about it all the way through. "This is what I get for messing around with things we don't really understand. Take heed, Bob…" Those were just about the last words she spoke to me before she went into a coma at the end.'

'What about Miranda's mother—was she around?'

'No—they'd fallen out in a big way over me, especially after Maddy had me move in, under strict conditions around her work I should say. I had to be off to college each day by eight, bring her coffee before I went and not engage her in morning conversation lest she lost the night's images. That's writers for you. It created a family scandal though. There were big screaming matches about how she'd pinched her daughter's boyfriend, had it planned all along and so on. Pretty passionate, that family.'

'So you were the one there for her?'

'Mostly. Anthony would come in sometimes, and he was very kind to both of us. Still is to me—still keeps in touch. And I had a weird sense in the last days, when I was in there with her holding her hand and talking to her. It was a feeling that her consciousness was fully present. She couldn't speak but she was watching. Her eyes were open. Right at the end, when the doctor came round and read her notes, he checked for the vital signs and knew they were failing, knew she was in discomfort, so he reached down and turned up the morphine pump—surreptitiously, like they do. I was watching her eyes. They'd been shut but opened and dropped down to what he was doing, and then they looked up again and met mine. She'd logged it—knew exactly what was going on, didn't want to go, but she couldn't hold on any longer. The cancer had spread and her abdomen was swollen to fuck, belly tight as a drum with ascites. I saw the light go out of her eyes, and then her eyelids drooped and it was like another door shutting. She went that night, breath easing out like the touch of a butterfly's wings and then she was no longer there—just this solid, inanimate thing on the bed, like a statue, skin the colour of primroses.

'After the funeral Anthony, who was her literary executor, set me to work editing the last novel, going through her papers and putting them in order to sell to Berkeley, assembling collections of her stories and articles. She'd been the coming thing in her day and with dying like that so young, her stock soared—she's still big with the Women's Studies lot at my place. Another reason why there's been no-one else these last ten years—been too busy with all that, as well as the doctorate and then the lecturing at Birkbeck. And I got back into the climbing, in Pembroke especially—something about the quality of light on those white cliffs above the sea, the abruptness of them, the solidity of that sudden vertical rising from the swirl and motion of the waves—and the nihilism of all that was right for where I was at. Even the way you continually lose your friends I could cope with.'

'Jeez! I didn't know any of that. I can sort of understand now why you haven't been with a woman since. Look out—here's where we have to pay to get into Wales. Got any quid coins? Note that they don't charge you for leaving again. How are we to deconstruct this particular pecuniary ploy on the part of government?'

'That you can cough up for the privilege of being here, and then the Welsh are so glad to see you go you can get out for free? We should make the pub in Bosherston in plenty of time for a beer or two.'

We arrived on the vicarage field campsite in the last of the daylight and bumped across the ruts to the far corner. There was a sleek blue dome-tent already on the choice pitch, with a little teal blue M.G. Midget alongside it. I pulled up twenty yards away and Nicky started heaving stuff out of the boot.

'How come you've brought three tents, Nick?'

I'd brought a tent anyway, knowing from past experience what was likely to happen.

'One for me and two are special orders—I'm just deciding which I'll use.'

'You'll get caught one of these days at that trick.'

'*Alpine Adventures* can afford it—rich bastards. I'm just sharing out their profits among the deserving poor of British climbing.'

'And taking a cut yourself whilst you're at it? Sure you're not giving in to the less worthy motive of gaining revenge for the pittance they pay you?'

'Don't complain—it'll pay my share of the petrol down here. And I'll buy you a pint when we've got the tents up. I'll go this side the car so that if I get lucky in the pub I won't keep whoever's in that other tent awake all night with the shrieks and howls and unworldly gurglings a woman is wont to make in the transports of passion. Or at least when she's with me.'

'Come on, Casanova—you're more impressed with yourself than Fran seemed to be the other night. And I hope you get some sleep tonight for what we've got in store tomorrow.'

'Spoken like a true monk. Now let's stick the tents up and slope across to the pub.'

The St. Govan's Inn was deserted. We walked in, Nicky said, 'I'll get these,' and eased over to the bar, so I sat down at a table, noticing that the next one was already taken, a handbag on the seat, a book and car-keys on the place-mat. I looked up and saw the woman from The Crown emerge from the ladies' and walk over.

'Thought I might find you here—deductive reasoning!' she said, putting the car keys in her bag and moving the book—Mauriac again. I registered it and must have looked quizzical.

'Great thing about Catholicism—if you say you're sorry you're forgiven. Sorry I disappeared so abruptly on Wednesday!'

'Thanks. You're forgiven. Though I doubt there's any need and you haven't got that quite right. It's if you express contrition and perform penance you're forgiven. But you know—I doubt there was even venial sin involved in your departure, so you don't actually need to confess. And it's my turn now to be sorry, for getting in deep.'

'Deep as you like,' she came back, that half-smile present. I knew how Bogart must have felt when he met Bacall.

We ended up talking all evening. The Crown crowd started arriving in dribs and drabs. Nicky homed in on a woman I'd seen at the Mile End Wall once or twice and was soon in world-occluding conversation with her at the far end of the bar. About ten o'clock I was fading. It struck me that the brown-eyed woman and I still hadn't introduced ourselves, conversational topics and intensity not having allowed the space.

110

'Where are you staying?' I asked.

'Over on the vicarage field.'

'In a blue tent with a little M.G. alongside?'

'That's the one.'

'Then I'm right next to you.'

'In that case, I'll walk you home. You look done in, and I'm about ready.'

Nicky caught my eye as we were leaving and gave me a salacious wink that I studiously ignored. Outside in the dark she linked arms and we wandered into the field. I liked the feel of her against me, the fit and the rhythm of our bodies. We leant close. A few more tents had sprung up nearer the gate.

'My name's Jan,' she said.

'Mine's Bob.'

'I know. Angie told me after I saw you in the pub on Wednesday. She asked who'd been there in The Crown. I must just have a pee. Wait for me.'

She went across by the wall and rejoined me outside my tent.

'I've a half-bottle of Jura in mine if you want a nightcap.'

She took a step in that direction and turned her head to see if I was following. A car was driving into the field. She was caught in its headlights. As if for the first time I saw the trim shape of her, the watchful intelligence in her face, the dark cascading hair. I followed. She lit a candle and we sat on her sleeping bag and *Thermarest*. Bottom in my face, she searched around in a box, uncorked the whisky, measured it out into Greek glasses—'Can't drink good malt out of plastic mugs!' —and handed one across. We clinked.

'Am I right in thinking…' we both began.

'Yes,' she answered, pulling me to her and clinking glasses again before kissing me on the cheek, and then more lingeringly on the lips.

'I'm a bit out of practice.'

111

'Does it take practice?'

'I seem to remember that's what makes perfect.'

'I'll settle for less right now. Go get your sleeping bag and a mat—might as well be comfortable.'

She pushed me out of the door. By the time I returned she was already naked. She zipped up the tent before she unzipped me.

We rescued our glasses again and sat watching each other in the candlelight, glad of our nakedness at last.

'You were Maddy Perceval's love-interest, weren't you?'

'At the end, yes, if you want to put it like that.'

'I just found out. Checked out in the library at my place. I loved what you wrote about her in those introductions. You were so young then. Come here and kiss me again. Something tells me you need a woman right now. And I could sure do with a man.'

'Seen one you fancy, then?'

'Quit the wisecracks—you'll be tuning up the guffaws next. And don't worry. I'm quite safe at the moment. You're not going to end up paying child maintenance, though I might turn into some pre-menstrual Gorgon in the night.'

Nicky's voice brought me spiralling up out of the depths of sleep.

'You in there, Bob?'

'Yes.'

'I'm off over to Ma Weston's for breakfast. No hurry. Low tide's not till two—it'll be after mid-day before we can get on to the route.'

He went off singing to himself. Jan's head was nestling in the crook of my arm.

'Hey lover,' she breathed, 'don't move yet a while. Or if you do, make sure it's in my direction.'

An hour later she nuzzled at my ear.

'I know you're going climbing with Nicky today. It's OK I've arranged to go over to Bow-shaped Slab with Angela, so see you back here later.'

'Was that the woman Nicky was in deep conversation with last night? I didn't know her name.'

'Or shall we call it intercourse?'

'Who's wise-cracking now?'

'Yeah, but I still can't guffaw. And yes, it is her. She's a student of mine at Holloway.'

'You women have got it all sewn up!'

'Now you know that's not true.'

Eventually, much later, we made our way over to Mrs. Weston's.

'Tea, and poached eggs, is it? Well, been a long time since I saw you, my dear,' Mrs. Weston said to Jan. Her hair and make-up was immaculate as ever. 'Not this chap, mind. Can't get rid of him. Always down. Nothing better to do with himself.'

She bustled off into the kitchen. Nicky and Angela were at the big table and we joined them.

'I gather our plans have already been made for the day,' I said to him.

'Our plan stands, just for today. See how we get on and who knows what tomorrow holds. Are you feeling up to it?'

'Sure. Never felt better.' Jan squeezed my thigh under the table. The poached eggs arrived. An hour later Jan and Angie had raced off in her Midget round to Stack Rocks, and Nicky and I were ambling along the cliff-tops, skylarks singing and the sun shining, heading west, a few white crests on the sea neatly counter-pointed by delicate riffs of white cloud. It was already slack water, an oily sea sluicing and sucking gently in and out of the zawns. Out of bravado Nicky picked up the shells lying about and hurled them against the rusting corpses of tanks on the firing range. 'Ka-boom! Ka-boom!' he shrieked, like a five-year-old playing war-games.

'Did I tell you about the sheep when I was down here in October?' I asked, to distract him.

'No, go on—is it a long one?'

'Yes, if you want it to be.'

'So what were you up to with this sheep? Is it as good as the story of Pete Minks on the Paine expedition? We've got a copy of the photograph up on the notice-board at work.'

'This is a decent, moral tale.'

'OK—I'm bored already.'

We were nearly at the cliff so I didn't bother. Both of us were anxious about tide times.

'How long d'you reckon you have, to get on to the lines down there?'

'An hour for slack water, and maybe half-an-hour either side. The tide just races through the channel beneath the cliff and the inward-tilted slab as soon as it starts to turn. No way back once you're on the rock—it's up, or sit it out till the next low.'

'Not good—we'd miss the pub. And whatever else was on offer.'

'Well—so long as they didn't call out the rescue. Can you imagine the shame! I'd never show my face in The Crown again. Imagine the onslaught from all those guffawing buffoons! You'd drown in exhaled beer-froth.'

We slung the sacks down on the terrace by the abseil point, sorted out our racks, pulled on rock-shoes, laced them just so and set up the descent rope. I never let anyone else do that, not even Nicky. Too many friends dead. I stepped over the edge, let my weight cautiously on to the belays then slid down to the base of the cliff, where I unclipped the figure-of-eight and shouted up:

'OK Nicky—I'm down.'

Eager to see what we were letting ourselves in for, I skipped across boulders and dodged waves that were sluicing around in the end of the channel to gain the slab. The cliff was overhang-seamed, south-facing, only two obvious entries through the viciously undercut lower section. The slab gave a grandstand view of what lay in store. After a couple of minutes' route-study—contemplative, curious, piecing the features together, wondering what rewards and surprises intimacy would bring—Nicky was bounding up the slab to join me. He turned to look at what we'd come for, and let out a deep breath.

'Wow! Whichever first pitch we take is your deal, I reckon. You're into the brawny stuff. I'll have that long slanting groove offset to the left that comes next—looks more my style. Tricky Nicky to the fore on that bit!'

Above the wave-smoothed channel the first sixty feet of rock jutted out at an angle twenty degrees beyond the vertical.

'You can quite see why no-one's bothered before now,' I said to him.

'Quit gabbing and get on with it—I don't want to drown!' he retorted, handing me the ends of the two ropes.

'I think we'll do the one on the left. There looks to be better gear on that.'

He put my ropes into his belay-plate and I pulled up on to a block sticking out at the foot of the crack, squatting on it and sorting out the wired nuts on my rack, counting the quick-draws on my harness in some sort of nervous ritual. I fiddled a big nut into a good slot at arm's reach overhead, clipped a rope in, looked down and nodded to him. A quick exhalation of breath and I was swinging out on to the bulge above, revelling in all the automatic adjustments of the body: the roll of the shoulders; the foot-push to get my next stretching hand on to a hold; the running-up of my feet across blank rock and the turning-out of a knee to get the toe just so on a square-ish little block of limestone; the instant of hanging there, viewing what was above, sizing up, energy coiling taut as a spring, and then the long, timed move up and past and through, the awkward half-secured tentativeness of a hand searching for a jam in the crack and the relief as it locked immovably into the secure place.

I clipped another runner, and by the ease with which the right rope came through I knew he was with me, alert, attentive. In an ecstasy of my own strength, I raced up the crack to the lateral break at sixty feet, sidled out left to a comfortable niche with perfect belays in its back, tied on and brought Nicky up to join me.

'Well done, youth,' he grinned, patting me on the knee as he arrived at the stance. 'If it all slips into place like that we're on to a winner. Might even get another one done today!'

'Not with the tides…'

'I wasn't thinking of here.'

The air on the face was very still, the sun just beyond its zenith baking, the heat reflecting from the white rock intense. I gave him the gear he needed and nestled into the niche, legs hanging out over the edge.

He'd turned edgy and uncommunicative, was craning his neck to scan the way ahead. He fumbled in his chalk bag and marked the dimples across a smooth band of rock in the slim groove that led out from the stance, then tested the minuscule finger-edges, whistling air out through his front teeth, stepping up to fiddle a couple of small wires into a thin crack in the back of the groove, clipping quick-draws into them and tugging to test their security.

'Good!' he said, glancing back down. 'They're solid. You quite comfortable in there?'

'Oh yeah—might catch up on a few hours sleep if you're going to take as long as usual.'

He gave my shoulder a playful prod with his toe and started to move, neat and smooth as ever, rock-shoes precise on the smears he'd marked, hips thrust forward into the groove to keep his weight off the finger-edges, reaching over the bulge above and skipping rapidly through as I drowsily paid out the rope and he disappeared from sight.

I imagined him up there, on a small foot-ledge with an easy groove, samphire growing in the back of it, leading ahead. In my mind he was looking for protection, trying nuts in flared cracks, giving up and moving rapidly on. The rope ran out in jerks of quick movement. He arrived at the foot of the steep band of compact rock we'd seen from below, came to a halt scanning it, tried to place a runner at his feet but it lifted out of the crack and slid down the rope.

He was feeling the tiny finger-holds by which to start the sequence up the wall. Already he had eighty feet of rope out. Thirty feet above him a straightforward corner ran to the top of the cliff. He stepped up on to a good, sloping foothold that made his calves ache. Four or five long moves would take him to a good handhold below the corner. He dabbed chalk on the footholds he might need. To fall from here would be terminal—fatal splashdown in the channel beneath, which was already surging with water. He felt at the fingerholds that began the sequence, arranged gear on his rack for a thin crack that a couple of tenuous moves would bring within reach. The lack of protection frightened him. He let his weight back down on to the long foothold and relaxed, studying what lay ahead, breathing deeply in and out. Then he was ready.

He flattened on the rock, pointed like a ballet dancer to gain an extra inch or two of height, crimped his finger-tips on to tiny edges. A ripple of tension ran through his body. He convulsed upwards, kicking his feet out and running up the wall to place his left toe precisely on a fragile, sharp nubbin the size of a thumbnail. Locking off on his left arm he reached through for a pocketed finger-jam at the base of the thin crack, laying away off it, swivelling his left knee out, rolling his hips over the foothold so he could semi-rest and fiddle a wire-nut into the crack above.

The rope came easily as he clipped the runner. He backed it up with another, straightened on the foothold, left arm shrieking lactic outrage, right still not able to reach the hold below the corner. The top runner was now at eye level. He slipped his right toe awkwardly into a shallow pocket alongside his left thigh, eased his left foot off and canted his leg out to keep balance. All his hopes now focused on the hold just above. Every scrap of timed awareness went lunging for it. Fingers snatched on to it— flat, rough, matchbox-sized. Should he go on it?

There was a foothold out left if he could only change hands. The rope had begun to drag. He tried to adjust his right foot in the pocket, so he could get his balance, change hands and reach through. He felt the fretted edge of the pocket crumble under his foot, grabbed for the security of the runner and it pulled out, the one below likewise as his weight came on it. His limbs cartwheeled and cascaded down, on to the slab beneath, lancet rock carving his flesh as its bulk crushed his skull and thrust him outward flailing into helpless air.

The sudden jerk on the rope roused me.

'Slack, you bastard—you gone to sleep or something? We're there. I'm in the top corner, about twenty feet to go. Loose from here on but OK Pretty technical, that last bit…'

Soon the rope was running out as he took it on top. I untied from the belays and set off following the long pitch.

'Great route, Nicky—good lead! Glad you had that bit…'

'Yeah—had you nodded off down there? Just at the critical moment, and I couldn't get an inch of slack? I was yelling at you, screaming for slack…'

'Oh, I was just day-dreaming—thinking about last night…'

He rolled his eyes. 'I suppose you're allowed, after ten years without. Anyway, you nearly had me off, which I wouldn't have appreciated. That gear was crap by the crux. I'd have taken a monster. Stay alert next time, will you…'

We didn't climb together next day. When we arrived back in Bosherston Angela and Jan were sitting in the sunshine at a table on Mrs. Weston's lawn, a pot of tea between them, early wasps zipping around.

'I'm borrowing Nicky tomorrow,' Angela said, eyes fixed on him. 'I thought you and Jan might appreciate the time.'

'Fine by me,' he responded. 'This dozy old git could do with a rest after following my superhuman efforts today.' I said nothing, exchanged a discreet pleased look with Jan. Later we walked down by the lily ponds to Broad Haven and swam in the sea. Come the morning—the late morning —we lazed over to Gun Cliff, roped down the brief wall from those mysterious rusty rings and sat a while on the terrace at its base.

'I found a camp here once, right where we are up above high-tide level—sleeping bag, clothes, a primus. I was down for a week climbing on Mowing Word and Stackpole. Nobody came. Something about it felt very amiss.'

'Did you tell the coastguards?'

'Heavens, no! You didn't go near authority in those days. None of us would've done.'

'Who do you think it might have been?'

'Drugs? I.R.A? No idea. Whoever it was knew the coast. Then one day it was gone—not a trace.'

She took my hand and held it. We raced across the beach of the inaccessible cove, leaving footprints in unmarked sand, squirmed through the inside route that leads out on to the west face of Mowing Word, climbed some of my favourite routes on that glowing, magnificent headland—*Heart of Darkness, Flax of Dream, Logos*. I was peering down from the belay on top as she drifted across the toe-traverse on the third pitch of *Flax of Dream*, right on the lip of the void, poised in space, beneath her the massive overhangs and the leaning wall above the cave, waves surging rhythmically far beneath into its shadowy entrance, harmonizing with remembered waves in her own body, drawing him in, she in perfect balance, rough surety of stone against the fragility of flesh. She was so calm and absorbed, climbed with neat, sure economy and grace—competence too on the pitches she led. And she was at one.

'You've got a gorgeous arse, d'you know that?' I called up an hour later, as she reached the little pedestal on *Logos*.

'Know what the difference is between a man and a woman?' she returned. 'This is it. A man falls in love with a woman for her arse, a woman with a man for his mind. So you're running true to blokish form.'

'Are you making some large, unwarranted assumptions there?'

'Yes, and I reckon I'm right. I know my signs, "dozy old git." But you're quite safe 'cos I'm heading along the same path. You know what Saint-Exupery says about love not being to do with gazing into each other's eyes but looking together in the same direction? And as to unwarranted, you know love comes with no guarantees. I'm not sure climbing isn't the safer activity.'

She eased up that rickety top wall that looks as though it's made of crumbling concrete. We lay in the deep grass with the thrift and the squills, coiling the ropes, watching a seal watching us.

'I need to be away mid-morning tomorrow—want to beat the holiday traffic coming back into London. I've a new lecture on Mauriac that needs to be ready to give to the third-years when we start back.'

'When shall I see you again—assuming you want to see me?'

She pinched my calf, prodded me softly in the ribs and ruffled my hair by way of response before hauling me back prostrate on the grass, slipping out of her shorts and easing herself down on to me.

'Happy now, little man in there? I'm not your smugglers about to do a disappearing act you know. And if you've got abandonment issues, I can cope with them to a degree and so can you. I have to go to my folks in Exeter next weekend so I'll be off down the M4 again on Friday straight from work—it's their ruby wedding and they're a right pair of fond old sentimentalists. I wouldn't miss all their soppy stuff for the world. Bit early to introduce a new bloke—I'll just warn them there's one in prospect. There's not been one for a few years now, so they'll be pleased. And inquisitive, if not inquisitorial. So to answer your question, come to dinner at my place a week Tuesday. Come early so we can go for a walk in Kew Gardens.'

'Is that where you live?'

'Yes. It's handy for the commute out to Egham. I've a flat on Holmesdale Road. It's off on the left just after Victoria Gate. 27a. So we're not that far apart. Can you make it for 6.30?'

'Yes. How do you know where I live?'

'Angie told me.'

'You two know everything…'

Satisfied, she slumped down on to his chest, listening to the steady resonance of his heart within its cage of ribs.

'We tell ourselves stories to go on living,' she mused to herself. 'How does this story with Bob pan out? Do I have the courage? To hold to the narrative and live it through?'

From this time she remembered back to that place: to her years with Ferdie Turton; to his tenuous interface with the acceptable, with social behaviour; to the torrent of ideas and language in which they had mingled; to his agonizing descent into schizophrenia; to the last days, and her finding him in the wood. Barely conscious of doing so, she was breathing out lines of a poem:

> *'Nothing in the world is single,*
> *All things by a law divine...'*

Stirring beneath her, he heard, continued:

> *'...In one spirit mix and mingle,*
> *Why not I with thine?'*

'Not sure Shelley's always the best example to follow in these matters—I was thinking of that, watching your mate Nicky yesterday.'

'He'll be alright—your mate's got the measure of him already, I'd say.'

'Good Roedean girl, that one, and she doesn't take being messed about. And nor do I, not that I think you would.'

It was a beautiful evening. I risked the parking wardens and stopped on Turnham Green Terrace, bought flowers and wine, turned up five minutes early and rang the bell. She opened the door of a neat garden flat, beckoned me in and leant against the door to close it. She took the wine and flowers off me and I followed her through into a light kitchen where she put the bottle in the fridge and asked me to reach a vase down from a high shelf.

'Men have their uses,' she smiled, and at last came close, put her head on my chest and her arms round me. I found myself shaking, ran my fingers through her hair, felt tears welling in my eyes. She looked up, kissed them away.

'Come on! We need some fresh air.'

We went out and walked across the road into the Victoria Gate, strolling along hand-in-hand saying nothing as we slipped behind the Palm House and along to the lake.

The sun was setting down-river, sinking towards the trees; planes were sighing past overhead, their undercarriages down; fat grey squirrels with scrawny tails lolloped around on the grass or stood on their hindquarters to peer. There was a bench on the bank, looking up to the memorial bridge that crossed the lake. It was bathed in low sunlight, the water in front of it burnished and rippling. We sat down. Jan was looking serious, anxious even.

'I've something to tell you,' she began.

She looked me in the eye, searching. Instinctively I knew what was coming.

'You remember I told you I was safe? Well I miscalculated…'

'You mean you're pregnant?'

'You men are so quick on the up-take!'

She said it teasingly, ironically, lapsed into seriousness again.

'Yes. I'm sorry. I did a test this afternoon. But I knew anyway. I've known since before going to Exeter…'

'You don't have to be sorry. Not in any way…'

I drew her to me, put my arms round her.

'And—how do you feel about it?'

'How you feel about it might be more to the point.'

'You first…'

She was biting her lip.

'I was terrified. At first I thought of never seeing you again. Thought it was far too soon. Felt dreadful about what I'd done. But I'd never realized until now that I'd gone on to tick-tock-time…'

I held her very close and she was crying into my shoulder.

'Don't you think most people arrive on this planet as a result of benign accident? What's to worry about in that? It's only calculated mendacity that would turn me off, and I doubt there's an atom of you would be capable of that.'

Coots were bobbing and jerking across the lake, diving suddenly and surfacing again, calling with that harsh, percussive note like a cold chisel glancing off rock, leaving ripples that spread across mottled gold. A Canada goose splashed down in an explosion of spray and a heron jabbed, quick as the blink of an eye in the shallows and came up with a minnow.

'I couldn't have a termination, you know.'

'Oh, Jan—I know. It would be unbearable. I wouldn't want you to. And the least important reason against it is that would be the end of us. I want there to be an "us". I want you, and our baby. What shall we do to celebrate?'

She flashed me a quick, warm look.

'Maybe it is too soon, because we don't "know" each other yet, except through our instincts and the rightness of our bodies together, and a few more scraps we might have gleaned from friends. But to say it's too soon, what does that mean? I know the politics, but isn't that just to lament the loss of power, of control, and when were they elevated to be among the virtues? It's the great thing about rock, isn't it—that it's continually facing you with the contingent made actual and immediate and urgent. And you've got to get through it with a degree of grace. I couldn't go through an abortion with any sense of grace. I couldn't do it anyway. I know it's a woman's right to choose, but I could never choose that. I think we often don't realize until it's too late how serious a psychic step that is. It's what Maddy wrote about in *The Ghost Child*, isn't it? Was that with you…'

I'd watched Jan the whole time she was speaking, felt her words drawing us together not as glue or artificial bond but in the way a craftsperson offers up, one to the other, the pieces that make a whole.

'No. It was with Anthony. It was what caused their split. He hadn't wanted it, told her to think of her career. I think he bullied her into it. She was only twenty-three, her first novel just out, he was her mentor so she went along with it. And maybe the regret was part of what killed her…'

We looked again at each other and then, hands clasped, turned to look along the path of the sun on the lake-surface, and the feeling was more perfectly peaceful than I had ever known. The way was laid out, and it shone.

Nicky arrived round unexpectedly at Abinger Road on Saturday afternoon.

'What are you doing in town?' I asked.

'I could ask you the same question. Anyway, I wanted to know if you were on for a trip down to High Rocks tomorrow. Maybe get Jan and Angie along? I fancy a vicious dose of snappy sandstone.'

'Can I get back to you on that?'

Next morning the four of us were clicking through the turnstile into the old pleasure-gardens by Tunbridge Wells. Nicky scurried around setting up the top-ropes and we went through the motions on *The First Crack*, *Coronation Crack*, *Renascence* and good old fingery *Tilley Lamp*. I was glad of the exercise, floundering good-humouredly on the old favourites, half-remembering sequences that demanded absolute precision, and that were already drifting away and out of memory. Jan whispered to me that she wanted to take it easy until three months, and she and Angie set out a picnic and teased at our competitive male flailings.

In the afternoon Angie and Nicky wandered off along one of the canyons between the boulders and became engrossed in an old problem-crack of Martin Boysen's, Nicky more attentive than I ever remembered having seen him. Jan and I lounged on a travel-rug, our backs to a sandstone wall.

'Do you mind, the changes all this will bring to your life?' she asked.

'What about the changes to your life?'

'We could just say our life? We can tell that story to ourselves and we can try to make it real.'

'What's real…'

'Our baby is. You are, I hope…'

'I want to be, for you. Something woke me up when I was in Pembroke, and it wasn't the climbing. Though that has its own reality—a dark one sometimes.'

'Good,' she said, nuzzling against me, and dozing gently in the warmth of the sun. 'Shall we call her Maddy?'

The Burning

a Jungian comedy of myth-taken identities

Yet how believe as the common people believe, steeped as they are in grossest superstition? It is impossible,—but yet their life! Their life! It is normal. It is happy! It is an answer to the question.
William James, *The Varieties of Religious Experience*

There was a thin, cold rain drifting in from along the river that late March afternoon, insinuating itself into the Vauxhall Bridge Road and the urban canyons of Pimlico. The young woman emerged from the tube station on to Bessborough Street, hunched herself into a black PVC coat and headed west along Lupus Street to drop a book back at the library. Droplets of moisture beaded her hair. She shook out her chestnut ringlets, caught the disapproving look and apologized to the librarian as she handed back the book.

'Tell Chomsky I'm finishing with him, will you!' she said with a smile.

'That sort of thing's best coming from you, darling,' retorted the librarian, wagging a finger at her in sly good humour, 'Always tell them yourself, and make sure you do it soon enough. Now do you owe anything on this?'

She was up-to-date with her renewals, took her ticket, turned her face back to the rain and pushed through the swing doors. Outside again in the raw damp, she headed off round the corner for the block of Peabody flats on Chelsea Bridge Road.

'God, I hate this place!' she muttered under her breath, looking up at dank brickwork and stained yellow walls as she hurried down the street and climbed the stairs to the flat. 'What am I doing here, and how soon can I get away? One more term and then…'

She fumbled the key out of her bag and into the door, squeezed through into the narrow hallway, slipped out of her coat and hung it on a peg to drip on old brown linoleum.

'Is that you, Beth? You're late today,' her flatmate called from the bathroom.

'Hi Rich! Yes. I did a shift at the Triangle. They're short-staffed till the weekend. Are you in the bath? I'm dying for a pee…'

'Won't be two ticks—put the kettle on and keep your legs crossed.'

'Ever practice what you preach?'

A loud raspberry by way of response. Bethan went into the kitchen, looked to see if there was water in the kettle. It was half full, to her relief. She switched it on and gazed out of the window at the tiny cramped balconies across the quadrangle, thronging with pots of herbs and flowers, bravely colourful in the dullness of approaching dusk.

'Want me to leave the water in?' Richenda called down the passageway, 'Bathroom's free now.'

'Yes, please—I'm freezing! Kettle's on.'

She slipped into the bathroom, relieved herself, wriggled out of her clothes and eased down into the bath, running more hot water before stretching out in contentment. There was a tap on the door.

'Tea, Beth?'

'Yes, please! Love some…'

Her flat-mate came in with two mugs, handed one to her, put down the loo seat and sat on it.

'What are you doing over the Easter holidays, Beth?'

'Hadn't made any plans yet. I don't want to do any more at the Triangle after this week. Need to revise for finals. How about you? Sounds like an ominous question.'

'Miles said he'd be down this weekend for the Boat Race. He said Cambridge are out for revenge and it should be really, really exciting. And there's a rugby match he wants us to see as well—Quins and London Welsh. He should've heard about his fellowship by the weekend too. There's a friend of his who might come with him if you're around—Jamie, he's really nice...'

'Are you trying to set me up again, Rich? Remember last time—that gorilla schoolmate of Miles'? I had to barricade my bedroom door. You and your public schoolboys...! He weighed about nineteen stone, had hair on his back, and slobbered when he talked to you. "Really nice," you said, "really, really nice—was at Repton with Miles..." Remember? Still, at least he wasn't a chinless wonder—he had about seven of them, as I recall.'

'Oh, Bimser wasn't that bad—especially when we persuaded him to put his shirt back on. D'you remember—you telling him his boobs were bigger than yours? Not true, actually...'

She reached over and gave one of Bethan's nipples a friendly tweak.

'Stop that, and soap my back. I have nightmares imagining what would have happened if I'd ended up beneath that.'

She sat up and handed across the soap. 'He was awful, Rich—anyway, if you're going to have the place full of loud, braying, overgrown schoolboys who stink the place out with their socks and farts and talk about nothing but rugger and how wonderful they are I'll just stay in my room and practice the violin...'

'I've a better idea. If Miles is around for the next fortnight, I won't need the Mini. You could take it up to Porthaur and practice there to your heart's content.'

'So you're trying to get rid of me. OK—what and where is Porthaur?'

'It's Mummy and Daddy's cottage in Cwm Blaen yr Afon. It's so lovely. We generally go up there for a week or two each summer, so it would be good to have it aired a bit beforehand. It's been locked up all winter. And it means Miles and I can make as much noise here as we like. Please, Beth! Come on—you're Welsh, you'd like it I'm sure.'

'I'm from Bracknell—you know, deepest Berkshire. It's my parents who're from Wales, and they never go back and they certainly never ever talk about it. It's like an unspoken thing between them. They got out. And would be horrified at the thought of my going there. Not that they need worry —from what I hear, Welsh boys prefer sheep to girls.'

'Definitely not true! I've been going to Porthaur since I was ten and I've had lots of fun there.'

She rolled her eyes and gave a big wink that her friend greeted with a stony face.

'Oh, you'd love it Beth. Will you think about it? You know how much you hate being in London…'

'Well—alright then. I'd rather be almost anywhere than London at the moment, so why not? Does it have running water and a proper loo and fires and things or d'you have to dig pits in the woods and wash yourself in freezing streams?'

Bethan set off early on Easter Sunday morning, before Miles arrived, in the lull between the Friday night holiday weekend traffic streaming out overladen and expectant, and the same families straggling back sodden and exhausted on Monday evening. Richenda handed her the car-key on a ring with a small, furry bear attached.

'I've put you on the insurance. Don't prang it, will you! Daddy would be livid with me. When you get to Cwm Blaen yr Afon, Mel at Cwrt y Cadno has the key. I've marked it on the map. She'll show you where everything is, or one of her sons will. You might like one of them—

they're really nice, but a bit wild. I sort of grew up with them, going there every summer. The oldest one, Elis, is married now, I think. Probably won't make any difference, though. Have you got everything you need? Toothbrush? Tampons? Mrs. Tiggy-Winkle? Yes? See you in a fortnight then. Phone me if there's anything you want to know. Or Mel will show you—she's really nice.'

'Even more really nice than Bimser?'

Richenda blushed. 'Yes. But she's quite witchy—now off you go. Miles will be here any minute and I've got to get ready—pluck my eyebrows, change the sheets, hide the evidence and all that.'

Beth gave an exaggerated grimace, asked how her skirt looked, and slipped into the coat Richenda held for her by the door. 'Thanks, Rich—and I hope you and Miles have a lovely time doing everything I'd never dream of doing.'

'Hope the rest of your gentleman callers stay away for the duration,' she added under her breath. They hugged briefly, and Bethan shuffled off along the landing carrying a bag, a rucksack, and her violin case. She stuffed the bag and rucksack into the boot of the tiny red car, put her violin behind the passenger seat, sighed appreciatively at the box of groceries and pile of sheets and towels Richenda had stowed on the back seat, and soon she was threading her way through deserted Sunday morning streets, heading out along Wood Lane, past Wormwood Scrubs and the cemeteries to the North Circular, musing on the prospect of a fortnight's isolation and novelty.

There was a solitary hitchhiker with a rucksack and guitar-case as she turned on to Westway by the Hanger Lane junction. 'He'll be safe enough,' she thought, and pulled in to pick him up.

'Where are you heading?' she asked, as he opened the passenger door and peered in.

'West?' he answered, with a quizzical smile.

'Me too—hop in.'

131

He placed the guitar case carefully on top of the piles in the back, folded himself into the passenger seat, rucksack on his knee, and Bethan eased out on to the road again.

'I'm Bryn,' he said, 'I'm heading for Aberystwyth, eventually.'

'I'm Bethan and I'm going to somewhere near Porthmadog.'

'Ti'n siarad Gymraeg…'

'Oh, that's Welsh, isn't it? What does it mean? My parents were Welsh, but they won't have anything to do with it any more.'

'Oh, sorry—it means 'd'you speak Welsh?' But since you don't, you'll have to put up with my English. It's not as good.'

She stole a quick glance at him—dark curly hair, brown eyes, an amused expression, strong hands, faded Levi's, a denim jacket—and liked what she saw.

'Do you live in London…'

They both spoke at once, laughed.

'After you,' he prompted, the voice surprisingly light and musical.

'Yes—I'm doing general arts at Goldsmith.'

'I'm reading law at Aberystwyth. I didn't want to leave Wales. My girlfriend's studying medicine at University College. I've just been visiting…'

'Damn!' she thought, and then, out loud, 'Law's for capitalist toads and lackeys, isn't it?'

'How about for fighting capitalist and colonialist toads and lackeys on their own ground? Is that a more hopeful view?'

A look of questioning and approval flicked between them. Her turn to smile.

'OK. Now, how do I get to this precious country of yours?'

'Oxford, Cheltenham, up the M5 to Worcester, then Leominster, Rhayader and the A470—it's the long way, but the one I go, out of aesthetic principle. And you don't seem to have been heading for the M1? You could drop me at Llangurig, or in Llanidloes or Machynlleth—I might be able to get a bus from either, though I don't know about Crosville and Easter Sundays...'

'Oxford it is, and then first stop in Tewkesbury. We can do your cross-country from there, but first I want tea and cake in the Abbey tearooms, and to see the spring squills in the abbey grounds. My favourite aunt used to live there. It was a family treat for us at Easter, visiting her. She had a little red-brick house on the road going down to the river from the abbey, by the side of The Bell.'

On empty morning roads past Oxford, Burford and Cheltenham they drove into clearing weather, chattering easily, fining down the narrative and editing the events of their lives to each other, sounding out enthusiasms and values, quietly evaluating physical presence from corner-of-the-eye glimpses, talking so freely they scarcely paused to draw breath. Before eleven o'clock Bethan was guiding the Mini into the car park by Tewkesbury Abbey.

'Let's go in and watch,' she said. 'There'll be a mass starting about now—very High Church, this old place!'

'They might not let a lapsed coalfield nonconformist like me in, then—the good respectable lord above might tell them that I'm a troublemaker.'

He enunciated perfectly, provocatively, rolling his 'r's and hitting his consonants hard, a teasing expression playing across his face.

'We'll sit at the back, and avoid their critical looks in that case. And I'll buy you tea and cakes afterwards to get you over the culture shock.'

She ran ahead of him along the path round the west transept, a slim girl in a long skirt, bright hair flying, and he was compelled to follow, a look on his face midway between disapproval and laughter until she turned, slipped her arm through his as he caught up with her, and pointed to the carpet of brilliant blue squills under the trees and across the grass. She looked up at him, they reflected each others' pleasure in the sight, and then hurried on into the great church, some admiring lines from a half-remembered poem by Hywel ab Owain Gwynedd flitting into his mind — *'Fy newis I, rhiain firain feindeg,/ Hirwen, yn ei llen lliw ehoeg'* — and as quickly cast out.

Crammed close into a pew by one of the massive pillars at the back of the nave, they watched as the service ended. Clergy and choir processed down the aisle, faces elevated and beaming with hieratic afflatus, to cluster in a small and inward-facing circle by the font as the congregation filed out.

'What did you think about that, Bryn?'

'I'd rather hear Cor Meibion y Rhos any day. This lot give me the creeps. Singing without soul or belly. And as for the rest of it, it's all about power and exclusion, isn't it? The English bourgeoisie at their old distinctions. God knows what Jesus would have thought of them. D'you know what Jung said about Jehovah? Or about the church, for that matter.'

'Tell me, you Welsh ranter, you,' she hissed, pulling down the corners of her mouth, giving him the hint to keep his voice down as fusillades of disapproving glances were loosed in their direction from priss-haired and brilliantined ranks sitting under the tattered and fading battle-standards hung high upon the walls.

'The trouble with Jehovah is that he thinks he's god, and the church is the projection of female animus. Hywel— that's my dad—says that in forty years time half of all Welsh vicars will be lesbians—not that there's any harm in that, of course!' he replied in clear and distinct tones, darting a look of playful challenge at Bethan and making for the door.

She followed, huffing to herself between indignation and entertainment, fascinated by his thickset elegance and confidence, her gaze relishing the swing of his slim hips.

'I don't think I'll be taking you home for quite a while yet, Master Bryn!' she shot at him, slipping her arm through his again as they made for the tearooms.

'I didn't know that was on the agenda. And what Joy would say about it if it was, I don't know either…'

'And you don't much care any more, do you? If I can put the clues together, you were on the road so early because she didn't come back last night. Just left you there in her flat wondering what she was up to. Except you knew, and with who. Is that right?'

He wheeled round, extricating himself from her arm, his face reddening.

'Yes, that's right, and no, you're wrong to think I don't care. I do. My family have looked after Joy from when she was fifteen. She couldn't stay at hers with her father the way he was. We had her live with us, and that wasn't easy in our house. I put off going to uni for two years, worked in Gwaith Jinks to see her and my sister through their 'A' levels and into medical school—Angharad's in Liverpool now. And Joy's off on the upward path without a glance behind for any of us. It's not just for my own sake, but my parents gave her so much, and ours is a close community. They're good people. They'll be hurt. I don't know how or what to tell them. So I'm not going back to Pen-y-cae for the rest of the holiday. I've an uncle who works in the extra-mural department at Aber and I'll see if he needs any tutors on the Wlpan courses next week…'

'Wlpan?'

'They're Welsh learners' courses. Total immersion in the language, based on what Israel did in Hebrew after the war. You should do one…'

She had stood back and watched his distress and confusion, and now she moved towards him again, linked his arm once more and gently drew him towards the tearoom. He didn't resist.

'So how come your father read Jung? He was a miner, wasn't he?' she asked, pouring tea into Willow Pattern cups.

'You mean miners aren't supposed to read? Is that a bit like saying it's OK to park in disabled spaces when you're out for the evening because cripples don't come out after dark? Your parents were teachers—what were their leisure interests?'

Bethan coloured up.

'Dad plays golf and mum is fanatical about bridge.'

Bryn looked at her steadily, eyebrows raised, lips pursed. She melted into a fit of giggles, kicked him under the table and they left hurriedly.

Somewhere after Ledbury a wrong turn took them into orchard country, rows of bare pruned trees on each side of the road, the apple blossom not yet showing, the Malvern Hills on their right descending into a region of wooded hangers east of Hereford with a mauve blush of coming spring across them.

'We used to come down here for the apple-picking in August, camp in a field behind the pub and work from dawn to dusk. Worcester Pearmains and Laxton's Fortune. Good money if you worked hard. All the Romany families would be here too. Lots of music and stories and dancing. I used to love walking up into the orchards in the dawn. There'd be white mist all across the Severn Plain and suddenly you'd come out of it into the sunshine and a world apart, perfect blue above and the hill-ridge standing clear like some great animal wallowing in the cloud-sea.'

'That's lovely. You Welsh! You all think you're Dylan Thomas. Did Joy like it too?'

'At the time. Not now. And what d'you mean, "You Welsh"? Listen, *Cymraes colli iaith*, your blood is Welsh, and now you're heading west. You might put two and two

136

together from what I've been telling you, but don't you think I might've been doing the same with you?'

'No—you're a man. Men never listen. They just bullshit and talk rugby. What d'you play on that guitar of yours?'

'What do you play on your fiddle? And by the way, Dylan Thomas is Anglo-Welsh. He's not a *Welsh* poet…'

She picked up on the edge in the last jibe and ignored it.

'Where do you know in those hills over there that's quiet? Then I'll play for you. The sun's shining. We can have a picnic. We'll see what Rich has put in that box of groceries. I know she put in a kettle and frying pan for Porthaur, and a little camping stove. They're under the seat.'

They sped out of Hereford along the Brecon road, Bethan putting her foot down, dancing the little car round the bends, getting the tyres to squeal, smiling to herself at Bryn's white knuckles as he gripped the edge of his seat.

'Right, we're in Wales now,' Bryn sighed as they rolled past Clifford towards Clyro, 'Sir Faesyfed—good old Radnorshire—the next English colony! The massed ranks of Hampstead and Highgate already on their way. There's a place quite close now in the hills where we can stop.'

At Llowes he directed her into a lane where stitchwort was in flower along the verges. It led steeply out of the valley of the Wye. The Mini laboured up the hill, clanked over a cattle grid and emerged on to a wide common.

'Take that track there,' he directed, pointing to a faint trail across the grass on the right. 'It's OK. You won't lose your sump or get stuck in mud!'

'It's not my car!' she protested.

They bounced along over green ruts, rounded a gentle shoulder where the first croziers of new bracken were unfurling out of a rusty litter of last year, and emerged at a copse of Scots Pine by the end of a long and sky-inflected pool.

'Here,' he pointed, and she drew up by a fallen trunk. They climbed out. Buzzards were wheeling and mewing

137

overhead; a sibilance of goldcrests flitted and wheezed between pines and bulrushes; two teal sculled across the lake and moorhens bobbed among reeds. Along the western horizon hill-ridges rolled in a fading succession, easing them round to the north and wrapping them in beyond the valley of the Bachwy.

'Oh my god! Oh my god!' Beth repeated breathlessly. 'It's just so spacious, so fucking gorgeous! And I never knew. I could get to like this country. You can breathe here. Don't know about the men, though—they seem a bit moody to me...'

She looked round for Bryn but he was busily gathering sticks beyond earshot.

'We won't need your stove—plenty of wood around,' he called across, then took out a Swiss Army knife, cut into the turf, rolled back a square and was soon breathing on a glowing heap of wood shavings, piling on more dry twigs as the flames leapt. She tucked her skirt between her knees and knelt by him.

'So, hunter-gatherer—go catch me a mammoth. We'll have mammoth steaks for afternoon tea.'

'Suppose I'm vegetarian?'

'Then bring back some dinosaur eggs and I'll make you an omelette. You still have them in this backward little country, don't you—dinosaurs, not omelettes?'

'Maybe I'm vegan...'

'Or even an ovi-pisco-lacto-vegetarian with carnivore tendencies? Anyway, I know you eat bacon because your jacket smells of it, so you're in luck.'

They brought the box from the car, made a camp by the fire, Bethan cut bread, melted butter in the pan and laid rashers of bacon to sizzle and curl.

'Sunshine, woodsmoke and frying bacon!' he said to her. '*Bendigedig*! How good is that? And you've even got H.P. sauce. There's luxury!'

'So what's this place called?' she asked, passing him a plate with bacon between two thick slices of bread.

'The Begwns—and over there are the Brecon Beacons. That scarp to the south, those are the Black Mountains above Y Gelli Gandryll.'

'What a mixture of Welsh and English!'

'It's border country here, fought over down the centuries, lines of old castle-mounds from Norman times down every valley.'

'What was that you called me in the car—rice-colly-nice or something? Didn't exactly sound like a term of endearment!'

'*Cymraes colli iaith*—a Welshwoman who's lost her language. Joy was the same. Wouldn't speak a word of Welsh even though it's my family's hearth-language and they took her in. People from England think we speak Welsh to exclude them. We speak it because it's our *heniaith*, our native tongue, the shape and expression of our consciousness. Can you understand that?'

She prodded his calf with her toe. 'Alright, mister—how about a hymn before the Sunday sermon? Finish your bacon butty and then get your guitar out while I make some tea.'

She went down to the lake to fill the kettle. He built up the fire for her to set it on, shaping the sticks to support, and sat down on the fallen trunk to tune his guitar.

'What are you going to sing?' she asked.

'It's a song by a friend of mine from Solfach. Beautifully written song about a lake, since we're by one.'

He began to sing, his voice unexpectedly clear and strong, ringing out, each word given weight as his fingers shaped a rippling melody from the guitar strings:

> *Mae'r blodau yn yr ardd yn hardd.*
> *Mae'r rhosyn ger y drws yn dlws.*

Ond nid yw'r blodau'n tyfu nawr.
Mewn ty o dan y creigiau mawr.'

He sang the lines plaintively, forcefully, deliberately, like a lament.

'Dwr oer sy'n cysgu yn Nhryweryn,
Dwr oer sy'n cysgu yn Nhryweryn…'

She picked up the refrain, descanted to it in a light mezzo-soprano, and he played it over and over for the pleasure of mingling their voices.

'So what's that about, Mister Bryn? What does it mean? You play and sing so beautifully I'm sure it must mean something very sad and profound.'

'We'll do it again with your fiddle, then I'll tell you.'

Except that when he'd played the song through twice more, and the fiddle had soared and swooped in and out of his playing, and once or twice as he'd watched how her long hair flew out across her shoulders and the way her breasts swung to and fro under her thin blouse in the passion of her bowing and fingering, he'd missed his own chords and quick laughing glances had passed between them until they both laid their instruments down on the greensward and, fingers touching aloft, they pirouetted in a flowing dance around the fire and then once more came to rest, sitting close on the fallen trunk.

'So here's what that refrain means—' cold water is sleeping in Tryweryn'—and he's contrasting that with flowers that grew in the gardens and roses that trailed round the doors of houses in the valley of the great rocks —and here's what it's about. A reservoir built within the last ten years for Liverpool that drowned a Welsh valley and its old community. So the flowers and roses and houses by the rocks are drowned now and the community gone. It's a kind of protest song and elegy all at the same time. I could show you the graffiti repeated by the roadside through Wales—*Cofiwch Dryweryn*—remember Tryweryn! There have been too many affronts like this to Wales. England looks on our land as resource to use or abuse as it will. But you know, be here for a while, come to know the feel of the land, get the sense of it in your blood. No point in my lecturing you now.'

He took up his guitar again, sat down by the fire, and finger-perfect now as he gazed steadfastly away from her and into the flames, played old Welsh songs to her —*Y Llwyn Onn, Cyfri'r Geifr, Clychau'r Aberdyfi, Cefn Ydfa*—some in plangent waltz-time, some rag-time, some helter-skelter, many with a soulful element of lament, and her violin followed him, talked to him, drew him out, explored and soared and danced along and around the known paths he followed.

'Excuse me!'

The voice plunged like a knife into their trance.

'Excuse me! Do you mind? You two there, you two — d'you mind!'

Bethan looked up at an angry blonde woman in a Barbour jacket.

'Do you know you're not allowed to camp here? No fires, no vehicles, no music. Didn't you read the byelaws on the back of the sign? There'll be bloody gypsies here next. I saw the smoke. I'm going to have to report this. I've got your registration number.'

'Oh, keep it, darling,' drawled Bethan in an affected accent Bryn hadn't heard before. 'You're most welcome. What part of darkest Surrey do you hail from, and what persuaded you to crawl out of it?'

'What did you say? What was that you said? How dare you be so insolent! We own property here and we don't want bloody plebs camping on our commons. My husband's a J.P. in Guildford—you haven't heard the last of this.'

'I'm sure no-one ever hears the *laarst* of anything with you,' Beth jibed, stretching the syllable to ludicrous length.

'Watch out that your roof doesn't get burnt from over your head one dark night, missus!' muttered Bryn. The blonde woman wheeled round on him.

'I heard that. I heard what you said. Making threats. I shall ring the police the minute I'm home and have you both arrested.'

'Tell them in Welsh and they might listen more sympathetically,' responded Bryn.

The woman snorted and turned on her heel, a plump yellow Labrador waddling after her with an air about it of phlegmatic resignation. Bryn and Bethan watched them go in silence.

'I didn't dare look at you,' Beth whispered to Bryn when she was a hundred yards away. 'What a cow! What a fucking bitch!'

'And I didn't dare speak. You were wonderful—*gwych iawn*! The neo-colonialists I told you about, stamping around in a cloud of entitlement to *our* country...'

'Still, if she's got the number we'd better go. It's my flatmate's car. I don't want to get her in any trouble.'

They heard an engine starting up on the road, heard it rev fiercely, wheels spinning, and then saw the Range Rover whine away over the ridge.

Bethan gathered their picnic together and packed it away in the car whilst Bryn took cups and plates down to the lake to wash them, stamped out the fire, poured water on the hot ash, and carefully fitted the turf back into place, patting it down and strewing pine-needles he fetched from under the trees across it so no trace of their brief presence could be seen.

'What a horror she was,' Beth said. 'D'you get many of them like that? I'm still trembling with anger at the cheek and the rudeness. Who the fuck does she think she is? Apart from the shithead wife of some Tory grandee from

Guildford, of course. Good job we didn't have a spliff on the go or we'd be in the Tower by now, in chains ready for hanging.'

'I thought I was supposed to be the ranter?' Bryn responded. 'Come on—she's spoilt it here, hasn't she. I'm sorry you had to come across someone like her. But there are more of them all the time. D'you remember that scene by the camp-fire in *Easy Rider*. What was it Jack Nicholson said? Something about what a good country this used to be.

She teased at his accent for the last sentence: "'...*hell of a good country*,'" she repeated. 'And it still is—we won't let her spoil it. Where do we go now?'

'That little road over there, the one we turned off, will take us down to Painscastle. Hope we don't meet her again on the way. Then we can go over Llanbedr Hill, along by Rhulen to Hundred House and down to Builth. We'll be back on the main roads then.'

'So what did happen between you and Joy, if it's alright for me to ask?'

The question that had been nagging at her slipped out as they climbed over Llanbedr Hill and the single-track road levelled out among the heather.

'Let's go sit down by that spring and I'll tell you, if you really want to know.'

'I only want to know if you want to tell me.'

Bethan pulled the car off the road and they walked silently down a green lead through the heather to where the spring bubbled up from between stones in a rushy bottom. Bryn scooped up water in his hand and drank.

'Try it! It's so cold. Delicious too...'

She stooped to drink. He squatted alongside her in the heather, staring intently at the ruins of a nearby farmhouse, avoiding her eyes, tears in his own.

'She just went off with someone. I don't really blame her. And she took longer about it than most of the medical students. She told me in the first week the girls had all gone on the pill and they were hopping from bed to bed like rabbits on speed. But she wasn't, or so she said. Though she was very distant when she came back at Christmas— distant with all of us. We'd arranged before she left that I'd go to London at Easter, but I don't think even then she wanted me there. She was just playing along with it, avoiding a scene—a lot of tension between her and my mother. Those two never really got on.

> *'The breath of her false mouth was like faint flowers,*
> *Her touch was as electric poison,—flame*
> *Out of her looks into my vitals came,*
> *And from her living cheeks and bosom flew*
> *A killing air, which pierced like honey-dew*
> *Into the core of my green heart.'*

'Shelley?'

'That's right. 'Epipsychidion'.'

'Not bad for a would-be lawyer!'

'Or for a collier's son from Pen-y-cae?'

'I wasn't thinking that.' She leant towards him, put an arm round his knee and rested her head upon it. 'So what happened yesterday?'

'We got up late. Had breakfast in bed. She went out shopping in the afternoon and said she'd be back around five and we'd go out to see *La Regle du Jeu* on the Portobello Road. I was going to do some revision. I moved a pile of papers, her college stuff, to make room on the table and a postcard fell on the floor: "Joy! Yo! Thanks for last night. You're the best shag in the universe. Hope you need a good seeing-to again some time soon! Let me know when. Rob." That was all it said. Date was a month ago. She didn't come back. I think she'd left it for me to see. So I left when it got light, took the tube from Shepherd's Bush and you know the rest. And thanks…'

144

He put an arm round her shoulder, gave it a squeeze and ruffled her hair.

'It's been my pleasure—so far. Had we better push on, before another harridan appears from nowhere to harangue us?'

Back at the car she scuffled around on the back seat and drew a road atlas out from under the boxes.

'Show me where we are and where we're going.'

He pointed out Builth and Llangurig.

'Look!' She jabbed with her finger. 'We could carry on heading west past Beulah—that's out of Blake, isn't it?—and take that funny little wiggly white road with all the arrows through what's that name…'

'Pontrhydfendigaid,' he obliged, 'it means "the bridge of the blessed ford".'

'…then I could drop you at Aberystwyth. How does that sound for the lift of a lifetime?'

'Gwych! Ardderchog! Ffanastic iawn! But it's a horrible drive for you, and Aber's still two hours away from Porthmadog. You'll be exhausted…'

'I'll take that chance.'

She drove slowly, in a state of rapture, through the vast, empty expanse of hills. Dusk was coming on, rabbits caught in the headlights, as the Mini rolled down out of the forest after the rough crossing by Hirnant and Cefn y Cnwc.

'I'd no idea it could be so wild. I don't think many cars will be coming that way again. I thought we were going to sink in those marshy bits. God knows what Rich would have said: 'I'm sorry, Rich—I had to leave the Mini in a Welsh bog!' I'm going to have to take it to the car-wash before I give it back.'

'You did well. I wouldn't have wanted to drive through that. Look—I want to show you something.'

They parked by a wall, climbed out and walked over cropped grass to an archway.

'What's this?'

He began chanting Welsh verse in response:

Mae dail y coed yn Ystrad Fflur
Yn murmur yn yr awel,
A deuddeng Abad yn y gro
Yn huno yno'n dawel.
Ac yno dan yr ywen brudd
Mae Dafydd bêr ei gywydd…'

'OK' She stopped him. 'Translation, please?'

'Your grandparents could have recited this to you—they'd have known it by heart. Everyone of their generation did.'

'But what's it about?'

'The sound of leaves on still nights; dead abbots keeping silence here. And Dafydd's grave—will that do to give you the sense of it?'

'No—but I get the impression it's all you'll let me have 'till I'm ready to learn the language. Who's Dafydd, and why's he buried here?'

'Dafydd ab Gwilym—he's our great poet—contemporary with your Chaucer, and a better lyricist. And he liked girls…'

'Glad some Welshmen do—I was beginning to wonder.'

'Come on!' he responded, a note of amused exasperation in his voice. They halted by the ancient yew tree. 'D'you want to hear some Dafydd…'

She nodded, fascinated and mildly irritated at the same time. 'Really, I'd like to be kissed,' she whispered to herself. He recited 'Yr Wylan'. She sat on one of the stones around the yew-tree and he asked if she wanted it translating.

'The sound's enough—it's so beautiful, all the sound-patterns, the repetitions…'

He considered explaining about *cynghanedd*, but thought better of it.

'How do you come to be able to remember all these poems, and in two languages as well, and you're not even studying literature?'

He looked at her as she was asking the question, caught the suggestion of a pout on her face, reached across and with two fingers gently raised the corners of her mouth, then leant close, put his arms round her, and kissed her on the lips. She snuggled into him, and he held her head, running his fingers into her hair.

'It's just the eisteddfod tradition—we're brought up with it,' he told her when they disengaged. 'It's all singing and poetry from as soon as we can speak.' He felt her shiver against him. 'You're cold, aren't you? Here, have my jacket.'

He took it off and draped it round her shoulders.

'Thanks! I've got my Afghan in the boot—it's a bit stinky, though.'

'My auntie and uncle live in Aber—let's go down there and get you warmed up. Are you happy with that?'

She nodded, and leant against him as he took her hand and they walked back to the car. He took it again as they sat and she readied to drive away.

'Beth, I like you very much. I think you're very attractive. But this time yesterday I was heartbroken about the girl I'd been with for four years. You know what they say about being on the rebound. And you don't speak Welsh—I'd be lynched at Pantycelyn if I'm seen with you…'

'Neither did Joy, and I can do better than her—I can learn! As to you being on the rebound, I can look after myself, thanks. And what's Pantycelyn, and make it brief, please?'

She let the tears flow as he put his arms round her again. He kissed them away.

'It's the Welsh hall of residence—we have to live in for our first year. Hot-bed of language politics. And all I'm saying is can we take it easy? I like you as well, fancy the pants off you actually. And we'll have some explaining to do at Uncle Huw and Auntie Angharad's. I hope you're ready for that.'

'I thought Angharad was your sister?'

'She is—she's Angharad Wyn. Auntie Angharad's my mam's middle sister. Angharad's named for her. They were the daughters of the conductor of Rhos choir. There's another auntie, the eldest sister on my mam's side, up north —Eleri Melangell. She married a sheep-farmer, but she's widowed now—met him at a concert in Smith Square when she was studying in London and he was down for Smithfield. I think she was at Goldsmith. Wales is like a big village, you know—the *Eisteddfod Genedlaethol*'s just an overgrown community fete. You and I, we're probably distantly related, and you can be sure Auntie Angharad will interrogate you, squeeze the last drop of genealogy out of you to find out. You wouldn't believe the amount of time she spends in the library doing her research. She'll find a connection somewhere way back. "Oh, so your mother was from Briton Ferry and your father from Pontardawe! And what was your mother's maiden name, *cariad*…" I can hear her now!'

Forty minutes later he directed her into a tree-lined avenue off the Llanbadarn Road and they pulled up outside a line of Victorian villas with neat front gardens. Lights were burning in a downstairs front room. She could see book-lined walls. Bryn rang the bell. A light came on in the porch, footsteps sounded on a tiled floor, and the door was opened by a slim, smartly-dressed woman, her dark hair flecked with grey, hazel eyes alight with intelligence and humour.

'Auntie Angharad, I'm sorry to be calling so late…'

'Brinley! What are you doing here at this time! We thought you were in London. And who's this with you? The poor girl looks frozen. Come in, dears, and I'll make some tea. Huw.'

She retreated into the hallway and opened the door to

the sitting room with all the books.

'It's Brinley, and he's brought a friend with him. Come through, dears, come into the kitchen.'

They followed her down the passageway into the warmth of the kitchen. His aunt pecked him on the cheek, then took Bethan's hand, holding it, rubbing the warmth into it and looking keenly into her face.

'Cold hands, warm heart! Yours must be a good one—these hands are like ice!'

'This is Bethan, Auntie—she picked me up when I was hitching out of London this morning and brought me here. She's heading up to Porthmadog.'

'Not tonight, she's not, Brinley! I'll make a bed up for you, Bethan, when you've had some tea. Brinley has his own room here. Now have you eaten? I'm sure you've not. Huw! Huw! Come and say hello to Brinley and his friend.'

She sat them down at the big, scrubbed table, took down a teapot from the shelf and warmed it with water from the kettle simmering on the Aga, placed willow pattern cups and saucers from the dresser before them and the filled teapot on a raffia-work mat.

'What will I get you to eat now? Sausages and eggs—will that do, *cariad*?'

She addressed herself to Bethan, who thanked her and said if it was no trouble…

'No trouble at all, my dear,' Angharad replied, a frying pan already on the Aga's hot plate and sausages dropping into the melted lard. 'Here's Huw, now. Huw, this young woman has had the kindness to drive Brinley from London today.'

'*Rhaid i ni'n siarad Saesneg,*' she whispered to him, and in the same breath carried on volleying questions at Bryn and Bethan as she bustled around rattling plates and cutlery and eggs and condiments out of cupboards and on to the table or to stand waiting by the cooker, and asking Bethan if she took sugar and milk and if she knew yet whether Brinley did, and of Brinley how Joy was, with a sharp look that grew softer when she received no reply but his downcast eyes. Huw, meanwhile—a slightly-built man in a shiny brown suit with long grey hair streamered down from round his bald pate, and a dreamy, distracted air—had shaken Bethan by the hand and greeted her, and had taken his nephew's hand and held on to it warmly before sitting down at the far end of the table to observe them both with mild and amused eyes from behind horn-rimmed N.H.S. spectacles.

'We came over from Abergwesyn, Uncle Huw—took the old road by Cefn y Cnwc that comes down to Ystrad Fflur. It's in a terrible state now, especially up above the forestry. I wanted to show Bethan Dafydd's grave.'

'Well I want to show Bethan some warm food and drink, Brinley—she's cold as the grave,' butted in Angharad, 'Now be a gentleman and pour the young lady some tea before it's too brewed. And be sure those sausages don't burn. I'll be back in a little minute.'

With that she scurried out of the kitchen, ran upstairs and they heard her in the room above opening cupboards and talking to herself. Within a couple of minutes she reappeared in the kitchen, checked the sausages, and turned to Bethan. 'Let me show you where you're sleeping, my dear, right above the Aga so you'll be warm, and where the bathroom is, and Brinley can bring in what you need from the car…'

Bryn looked from his aunt to Bethan, shaking his head fondly.

'Just the green bag from the boot, and my fiddle, please, Bryn. Make sure you lock it up, won't you?'

She handed him the key ring with the furry bear and followed his aunt upstairs.

'Here's the bathroom, my dear, just next to you, and Brinley's room is the one with the green door at the end of the landing. I'll get him to bring your bag up. So you're not from Wales, isn't it, but a Welsh name now, and you're Welsh as can be in your looks? Whereabouts are your parents from, then?'

In the space of a couple of minutes Angharad had Bethan's whole family history as far as she knew it.

'Oh, so your mother was from Briton Ferry, was it, and your father from Pontardawe! His father a solicitor, you say? And what was your mother's maiden name, *cariad…*'

Bethan smiled broadly at the memory of Bryn's imitation of his aunt.

'Now you freshen up and make yourself comfortable and come down when you're ready, *cariad.*'

When they came down, Bethan glowing after Bryn had brought her bag and violin upstairs and taken the opportunity to kiss her again and tell her how lovely she looked, Angharad was cutting and buttering bread, opening a can of beans and emptying it into a saucepan, slicing boiled potatoes from a bowl she took out of the fridge, and cracking eggs into the frying pan. Soon she was serving food out on plates and putting it in front of the young people. Bethan thanked her and without having been asked moved the H.P. sauce over to Bryn.

'Oh, so you know he likes that already!' Angharad nodded, observing every little gesture between the two of them as Huw watched his wife with a gentle incipient laughter. 'My wife misses nothing!' he commented fondly, as if of a favourite terrier.

When they'd eaten, and Bryn and Bethan had washed the dishes whilst Angharad cleared the table and put things away, his aunt made another pot of tea, put it on a tray with cups and saucers, milk and a plate of chocolate digestive biscuits, and directed her nephew to carry it into the sitting room, where she gestured Bethan to a fireside chair as Huw sat opposite and she and Bryn took the sofa.

'So where is it that you're heading tomorrow, *cariad?*' she asked Bethan, handing her a cup of tea.

151

'It's a place called Cwm Blaen yr Afon near Porthmadog. My flatmate's parents have a holiday cottage there. A woman called Mel at a farm called Cwrt y Cadno has the key.'

'*Esgob mawr*! Bless me! I can hardly believe my ears! Why, that's my oldest sister, Brinley's other aunt, Eleri Melangell. She's the mother of Brinley's three cousins. Did you know this is where Bethan was going, Brinley, and you bringing her this far out of her way!'

'Oh, no, Auntie Angharad—Bryn didn't make me go out of my way,' Bethan spoke up, 'In fact we've had an absolutely lovely day, apart from one little incident. We've had a picnic and played music together and been through the loveliest places I've ever seen in my life. And I'm so grateful to you for taking me in like this.'

The older woman smiled with pleasure at the easy way she used the form of address: 'You're welcome, my dear. Brinley's always been like a son to us, with not having children of our own. But are you expected up there? Will Eleri Melangell be waiting up for you? I should ring her and let her know where you are.'

'I'm not definitely expected today. My flatmate just told me to call there when I arrived for the key to Porthaur, that belongs to her parents.'

'That would be Richenda you're talking about, isn't it? Huw, are you listening to this?' Her tone was sharp.

Her husband had surreptitiously taken a volume of Parry-Williams essays from off the shelf, and now guiltily put it down and turned his attention back to the conversation.

'Bethan is the flatmate in London of Richenda, about whom there was all that fuss with Elis Wyn four or five years ago. Do you remember? Her father threatening because she was under age, and her the temptress all along. I didn't like that man, and I think he had a lot to do with how she was, *'ti'n gwbod*?'

Huw nodded assent, and Angharad ploughed on.

'Not the best of examples, your flatmate, I would think, but I'm sure it's not rubbed off on you, my dear.'

'Oh, Auntie Angharad, she's very kind—she lent me her car and the cottage.'

'Yes, that's all well and good; but those cottages are not things to be bought and sold, lent and borrowed. They belong rightly to the people of the community whatever the English property law might say, and it's sad when what goes on in them changes those communities for the worse.'

There was a hint of steel in Angharad's voice, hardness in her expression. Bryn slipped in to change the direction of the conversation.

'We had an unpleasant encounter up on the Begwns this afternoon, auntie—some overbearing Surrey *gast sais* who'd bought a house up there and resented our presence. Beth was magnificent, sent her on her way mightily offended. You'd have been proud.'

Angharad listened to Bryn's account and her features softened once more: 'I'm afraid you may find our opinions quite strong at times, *cariad*, but as you spend time in this country, as I hope you will now, you'll come to see why they've grown thus. I expect you're very tired, and heavens! it's nearly midnight. I'll make hot-water bottles for you, and then we can all be off to bed. Brinley, come and give me a hand.'

He went after his aunt into the kitchen, leaving Bethan by the fire with Huw.

'Now, Brinley, tell me what's happened between you and Joy?'

He gave her a brief, censored version of yesterday.

'Well thank heaven for that! Don't go chasing her now. Walk away with your pride intact, let that be an end to it. I know you've been fond of that girl and there's no arguing that away or explaining it, but she's used you and your family, and we won't be sorry to see the back of her. Joy indeed! Bad blood will out, and there's plenty of that on her side. Now this Bethan you've brought with you—she's cut from different cloth. I take to her, Brinley—and the way she looks at you is a pleasure to see. Not like that other cuckoo in the nest, forever putting you down and even getting your sister to side with her against you.'

She filled two hot water bottles from the big kettle, handed them to him and ruffled his hair.

'There then, *bach*, off you go—you and Bethan take it easy together and you'll both be fine!'

'Auntie Angharad,' he protested, 'We only met a few hours ago, and you're half way to having us married off already.'

'Well you know what Hywel would say about your meeting like that, and the timing of it. Synchronicity, he'd call it. That man has the best brain of all the ones we've married, always down the library at the 'Stiwt, always reading even as a young man, and not just Tarzan and Zane Grey like most of the rest of them. Huw has such respect for his mind, wanted him to go to Ruskin and do better by you all. Myfanwy would have supported him in that, and I know it's given her heartache, him staying down the pit. He's told me in this house—polite enough, mind, but no mistake!—not to interfere, and that his being down in the mine with the other colliers gives her the freedom on top.

"What's wrong with being a collier, Angharad *fach*?" he asked me, such an impudent smile on his face. You've got that way of looking too, Brinley. But he's a kind, decent man, your father, and he's kept Myfanwy happy all these years. They've a good marriage, those two; no-one can speak against it—love, laughter, lust and loyalty! There's the right mix! And I couldn't wish for a better brother-in-law. Better than that sly trollop Cadwaladr for sure—there was a sheep-farmer for you, to the life! An idle, sneaking lot with their subsidy tricks and Smithfield trips and drinking and womanising and all that. But don't go telling Eleri I said that—she's as proud as Hywel in her own way, and I know she felt demeaned by it, for all that he pleased her in the other way at first.'

She kissed him on the cheek, sent him upstairs to put the water-bottles in the beds, re-filled the kettle and set it on the stove once more then returned to the sitting-room fire.

'Angharad, sit down and listen to what Bethan here has been telling me. She's been studying English, music and linguistics at Goldsmith. What was it Eleri studied there—education and music, wasn't it? And Bethan's looking to be away from London after her finals. She's thinking of librarianship!'

Bryn came back into the room. 'Are you getting the third-degree from these two conspirators, Beth? Watch out, or we'll come down to breakfast to find they have our lives all planned out for us—you signed up for *Merched y Wawr*, me for *Cymdeithas Edward Lhuyd*, two more candidates for an emergent Welsh bourgeoisie, the rest of our lives a giddy round of cake competitions and nature conferences.'

His aunt pursed her lips and smiled. Bethan stood up by the fire. Angharad fussed across. 'Mind your skirt there with the flames, *cariad*! Lovely material!' She rubbed the soft cotton between her fingers, kissed her on the cheek and wished her a good night's sleep. Huw rose to shake her hand and she and Bryn climbed the stairs. Outside her room she put her arms round his neck.

'It's been such a lovely day, Bryn, I haven't laughed so much in ages, and your auntie and uncle are so sweet and kind. Your uncle's just given me a lot to think about.'

She kissed him passionately on the lips, pushed him away down the passageway and went into her room, closing the door behind her. Downstairs by the fire Huw and Angharad sat together on the sofa hand in hand.

'I'll talk to the admissions people at the college of librarianship this week, see how their numbers are for next academic year. What d'you think, Angharad?'

'No harm in finding out, isn't it. But you know, they've only known each other for sixteen hours, is it? We must be careful not to put pressure on them. Brinley's hurting from how the end came about with Joy—I can see that, whatever we might think of her. It would be unkind to press him into something on the rebound. But I'll ring Eleri in the morning and see if her boys need any help with the lambing this year. I know you had it in mind that he might tutor on one of next week's Wlpan courses, but something tells me he'd be happier up there with her. And I'm quite sure Bethan would be if he were—keep her away from those rampant nephews of ours too—she's far too good for the likes of them. *Hogiau'r Cwrt y Cadno* indeed! *Hyrddod* more like. They've the same morals as the rams they breed. No wonder Cadwaladr died of a heart attack. He was no better, and Eleri didn't have an easy time with him in that valley.'

When Bethan and Bryn came down to breakfast at eight o'clock next morning bacon was frying on the Aga, coffee was percolating and Angharad had the table ready laid. 'Good morning to you both. Sit yourselves down and did you sleep well? I always say a good breakfast will see you through the whole of the day if need be. Huw's out seeing about classes he's running up in Ponterwyd. He says goodbye to you both, and for you to come again any time, Bethan, with or without Brinley.

'Now Brinley, I've spoken to your Aunt Eleri this morning and she'd like you to go up there to help your cousins with the lambing. You'll be able to show Bethan the way. You can stay there of course, or you can stay at Porthaur if you're invited, whichever you choose, but remember this girl has to revise for her finals, and you've work to do for first-year exams, so I hope you won't be distracting each other too much. Work before play, as your *taid* used to say, and plenty of time for play when the work's been done.'

Half an hour later they were standing by the car, packed up. Angharad kissed Bryn, embraced Bethan warmly, and pushed a twenty-pound note into her hand. 'For the petrol, *cariad*. Now you're not to refuse, or we won't invite you again. Off you go then, and don't be so foolish as to neglect the work, will you! Whatever else you get up to…'

She waved them off down the road with a mischievous, glad look on her face.

They had talked and giggled their way through all his aunt's kindnesses and contrivances by the time the Mini was climbing out of Rhydypennau on its way north.

'So am I invited to stay, even though it's a while yet before I can meet your parents?'

He meant to joke, but it came out shy, hesitant. She reached across for his hand by way of reply.

'Try to stay anywhere but with me and I'll tie your shoelaces together, or something worse! You're mine now, and I'm not letting you go,' she hissed, eyes narrowed and teeth bared, more assured than him in attempting humour.

'That settles it, then. My dad says always to do as the woman asks, if you want a quiet life.'

'And do you want a quiet life?'

'I want a happy one. A useful one. A fulfilling one. How about you?'

'I'd settle for those three. D'you think they're possible? I wonder how our parents would score? I think my mum and dad still love each other and fancy each other. And they're both career teachers, so I suppose they've been useful. And they seem happy, even though what they do seems pretty humdrum to me. I'm not sure about some of their values now, but they've given me and my sister a good home and a safe upbringing. That's something to be thankful for, isn't it? My sister's a teacher as well, on a council estate north of Liverpool. She lives in a tower block in a place called Netherley, and her boyfriend's a plumber. I doubt if my mum and dad talk much about that at their golf and bridge clubs. What about yours? Tell me about Hywel—that's your dad's name, isn't it?'

'He's the best man I know—everyone says that about him. You can talk to him about anything; he's so attentive and naturally intelligent. And he's got a heart of gold. My mam used to be a bit frustrated that he wouldn't use his brain to get ahead, and was happy working down the pit. She used to nag him something terrible. But he's stubborn for what he thinks is right, and his political beliefs are just immovable. Our house has always had books and music and hospitality. They were the important things to both of them. That's how we came to take Joy in. I met her down at Wrexham library, brought her home, and when mam and dad found out what was going on at hers they invited her to stay with us and put a bed in Angharad's room for her, treated her as their own.'

'Did that work well?'

'At first. They're both such idealists they could never see trouble coming when it was obvious to everyone else. And if anyone had told them, they'd have been all the more determined to do good. Joy's father didn't help things by coming round supposedly to see her and making a pass at Mam. Hywel got to hear about it, went round to where he works and had him up against a wall, told him he'd knock his head off his shoulders if ever he tried that again. He's fierce strong, my dad, won't let anything pass if it offends Mam. They're great together, those two, and they're still like a pair of young lovers; the way they hold hands and sit close. They've been together since they were teenagers. Mam was going to be a teacher too—biggest export from Wales, you know. But she got pregnant first time she was back in Rhos from Barry and that was it—they had to get married in those days. I tease her about it sometimes; tell her how I was an accident. But I wasn't, you know. She looks pleased and embarrassed and sly about it all at the same time. She didn't like it away from home, wanted my dad, had seen what else was on offer out there, worried that she might lose him while she was away so she went and did something about it, knowing he'd do the right thing by her. I don't think she's ever seriously regretted that choice, and they take such a lot of pleasure in each other and what they do together. It will be terrible when one of them goes.'

'What was your mum's family like?'

'Her mother died giving birth to her so an auntie came to live with them, to look after the three daughters and keep house for Taid. He was pit head manager at Brymbo and conductor of Rhos choir. My dad sang in it, and he was winning all the tenor competitions at the local and *Urdd* eisteddfodau. He's still got a fantastic voice for all that he's never had training. He serenades her around the house and gives her fits of the giggles with what he gets up to. *Taid* was a nice old man and very fond of him. That's why there wasn't much fuss when he got her in the family way with me. Old Gwyn Talfan helped them a lot, setting up home and that. He bought them the house we're still in as a wedding present, even though he didn't own the one he lived in himself. He and Hywel didn't agree on politics exactly, with him being old Plaid and staunch for Saunders Lewis and dad a Marxist who'd argue for Saunders being a closet fascist just to wind the old man up. But they became great friends. *Hywel Dda* is what Gwyn Talfan used to call him. He was our great law maker in the tenth century, full of compassion, very modern in his view of the rights of women. I think the nickname fits my dad pretty well. *Taid* only died a couple of years ago. They raised a fund for a music scholarship in his memory at Cartrefle.'

'What a family you come from, Mister Bryn. I'm afraid you're going to think me very philistine and bourgeois by comparison.'

'Not from what I've seen so far, I'm not. And you don't want to be glorifying or mythologizing the way we are in

Wales too much—we do plenty of that on our own behalf, and it's not always realistic. I've a sense too that it will change within the next decade or two. Hywel's as critical as anyone of Rab Butler and Clem Attlee and Nye Bevan. He doesn't like the way personality cult subsumes political debate, especially in the press. But he's even-handed and sees the good things they brought about. What worries him is the effect a repressive bourgeois nation like England has within the union, and how easily all the hard-won victories on the part of the people can be turned back—even in little things like that last Tory education secretary, the one they elected leader last month, stopping free school milk. Hywel thinks she's a dangerous right-wing ideologue and fears for the effect she'll have on the working class. He says idealism's all well and good, but when you get an unscrupulous politician appealing to human selfishness and greed, the electorate's going to be lured down that blind alley.'

'I thought you said he preferred debate to personality cults?'

'You should argue that with him—there's always plenty of contradiction to gain you leverage in a discussion with Hywel.'

'Is that why you're doing law—all this tuning up to argue your cases before the magistrates?'

'Probably—I hadn't looked at it like that. But to come back to the practical effect of politics round us, the district nurse was round having a *paned* with Mam after Christmas and she was saying how it wouldn't be long before she'd be coming across cases of rickets again in Pen-y-cae, like they had in the 1930s. Hywel sees that minister's undermining of liberal state education as a reactionary counter-offensive against social ameliorism—as the start of another long war to re-affirm the hegemony of the wealthy and the public-school-educated, and protect the interests of capital. You'd have fun listening to the talk in our house. It'll be interesting to see how right my parents and their friends prove to be in the course of our lifetimes. And what our generation can do about it. I'm all for a socialist republic of Wales with Dafydd El as first president, but you know —'...*we were boyish dreamers in a world we did not know/When we walked to Merthyr Tydfil in the moonlight long ago.*' Maybe it is all moonshine, and vested interest will always be in control? I've just read that Marcuse *Essay on Liberation* and you can tell by the virulence of the attacks on him in the broadsheet reviews that he's caught the truth of the matter.'

She flashed him a warm look and slipped her hand along the inside of his thigh.

'Where were those lines of poetry from, my Welsh ranter—and what's a *paned* and who's Dafydd El?'

'You've had a *paned* or two already, *cariad*, to give you a clue—*paned o de, isn't it*,' he crooned, imitating his aunt.

'Oh, a cup of tea! And what about the poetry and Dafydd El?'

'Dafydd Elis Thomas—he's the *Plaid* M.P. for Meirionnydd Nant Conwy, good man of the left and he writes in *Marxism Today*. His father and my *taid* were great friends. Those two lines, they're from one of my dad's favourite poets, Idris Davies. He was a miner too from Rhymney. We grew up with his poems in our house— *Gwalia Deserta*, *The Angry Summer*, *Tonypandy*—knew all about the 1920s and that bastard Churchill before we were even in our teens.'

'Another good reason for me not to take you home just for a while. And by the way, if you're going to be staying with me in Porthaur we'd better stop somewhere and use this money your aunt gave me to buy some condoms, just in case your animal instincts get the better of you and you're ready to re-consider the warning you gave me last night. I'm sure Auntie Angharad would approve on all counts! She had a few little words with me this morning before we left. I'm not on the pill, and we don't want to go bringing any more little Bryns into the world by accident, do we? I'm not sure they could cope. Not sure if I can cope, if it comes to that, but we'll see.'

She glanced round and caught the distinct blush on his face before he turned to look out of the window.

'Gender collusion, is it! There'll be a chemist in Penrhyn —it's only a mile or so. And I'm not going in. I'm too embarrassed.'

'Leave it to the hard-faced woman then, you delicate young man, you,' she laughed. 'How many shall I get? A gross? Will that see us through the next fortnight? And clog up Richenda's parents' drains at Porthaur?'

'From what I hear, they'll be pretty clogged up already. She's had the valley boys queueing up for her favours these last few years.'

'Has she indeed, the little hussy! Just wait till I get back to Chelsea Bridge Road and hear what she has to say about all that.'

An hour later they were threading their way along the narrow road that followed the river into Cwm Blaenyrafon, Bethan stopping every few hundred yards to take it all in, asking Bryn about everything she could see. A gaunt old man in a heavy, belted coat with sergeant's stripes on the sleeves and hobnailed boots strode along in the middle of the road at one point and glared at them as she pulled in to let him pass.

'Who was that, Bryn?'

'They call him The Canadian. He lived over in Alberta for a couple of years in the 1920s, and then came back. He lives in the house built into the castle mound at Dolbenmaen, where the twenty-four hostages were given on the day Gwydion killed Pryderi. Never speaks to anyone…'

'So what's all that about the hostages?'

'Very long, involved story. Everywhere in Wales has its story attached. I'll tell you this one later, if you like.'

'I'll hold you to that.'

'I like the sound of the first bit.'

They drove on up the valley, parked in a lay-by and walked down to the deconsecrated church of Llanfair Blaenyrafon, under the rocky spur of Isallt, with its gleaming outcrops and its bluebell woods.

'Bryn, this is so utterly, entirely, incredibly beautiful! I'd no idea Wales was like this. Just wait till I talk to those parents of mine.'

'They're South Walians, remember—Briton Ferry and Pontardawe don't quite compare with what's here.'

'So who lives in this valley now?'

'There are still some of the old farming families, like my cousins, but the sheep-runs need economies of scale to be profitable these days, or scams like the double-subsidy. So there's many an old *tyddyn* gone for a holiday cottage by now, like Uncle Sion's.'

'Where's Uncle Sion's?'

'It's where we're going—Porthaur. It belonged to Uncle Cadwaladr's brother, and when he died they sold it off. Elis Wyn wanted to live there, but the rest of the brothers and sisters couldn't agree so it went to Richenda's parents. They paid less than two thousand pounds for it, but there wasn't the money in the family to buy it.'

'I've got more than that in a trust fund from my father's family. His father was a solicitor in Pontardawe and dad was an only child.'

'I wouldn't mention that at Cwrt y Cadno. There's still a lot of resentment, especially against your flatmate's family. Her dad came in and spent thousands straightaway on a new bathroom and septic tank, and Eleri's family still make do with washing in front of the range, and a *ty bach* over the stream. I wouldn't drink the water in this beautiful river if I were you, incidentally—I know what goes into it.'

They heard the sudden roar of a high-powered engine echoing between rocks where the valley narrowed ahead. A yellow car came racing down from between the jaws of the hills, slewed round the chicane over the narrow bridge with tyres howling and smoking, accelerated out of the bend and departed down-valley leaving a smell of burning rubber behind it.

'Mabon Rhwngddwyryd! Aunt Eleri will warn you about him. Come on—we'd better go and pay our respects and meet *Hogiau Cwrt y Cadno* if any of them are around.'

Ten minutes later, after turning off into a parallel side-valley and opening and shutting several gates, they pulled into a cobbled farmyard, farmhouse and barns on two sides and sheep-pens on the other, where the road they had followed came to an abrupt end. A tall, stately woman, her long dark hair tied loosely back with a red Post Office rubber band, came out of the farmhouse door. Bethan met her grey-eyed look, steady and unsmiling, and eased from behind the steering wheel to greet her.

'Aunt Eleri, this is Bethan…'

The sibylline woman turned her head towards him in brief acknowledgement.

'Brinley, the boys are up at the top barn. I'll take Bethan in and give her a cup of tea. You bring them down when you're ready.'

She waved him away, Bethan open-mouthed at the assured authority, catching at the quick smile and nod Bryn sent her in support before he vaulted a gate and set off running up the field beyond.

'Come on in, my dear, and help me make tea. How has your journey been? Angharad phoned again this morning after you left to let me know you were on your way. She said to send Brinley off to look after you in Porthaur—very wise, I would think. And you two only met yesterday morning, is it? Still, I'm all in favour of bundling, I wish I'd had the good sense, and she says you know how many sugars he takes in his tea already.'

'He doesn't take any, Aunt Eleri.'

The older woman turned and looked at her. 'So he doesn't! Best to keep him from bad habits, isn't it? And you don't speak Welsh yet? You'll be learning here. When I first came to this valley, hardly anyone spoke English. Just a few left like that now, and you'd be surprised at the knowledge they hold of the land. I've been collecting it this last thirty years. You need the language and all the knowledge it holds to treat the land here with right reverence.'

They were in the kitchen now. It was low-beamed, cured hams hanging from hooks. A tiny lamb lay sleeping on a towel in the warming-oven of the old cream Aga and a kettle simmered on the hot plate.

'How did you come here first, Aunt Eleri? Uncle Huw told me you were at Goldsmith?'

'I was. I studied Music and Education. You're there, aren't you, my dear? In your last year? General Arts, Angharad said, English, Linguistics and Music?'

'Yes. I'm hoping to revise for my finals whilst I'm here.'

'I'll keep my boys from pestering you, then, and make sure Brinley has enough work to do. I'm glad he's met someone at last who appears to be a decent young woman.'

The grey eyes travelled up and down Bethan and then looked straight into hers.

'He's a good boy, as they go, and his father a very good man, though he's pig-headed and obstinate and argues from dawn to dusk. That's what being down the pit does for you, I'd say, sitting around with all those other men, debating and ranting at each other with no women to keep a civilizing influence. I expect you've seen how his influence has rubbed off on Brinley?'

Unexpectedly, she burst into laughter, and Bethan joined her, the two women embracing each other and then spontaneously waltzing across the slate floor, Eleri taking the lead and both women singing a Strauss melody before Eleri disengaged by the Aga and in flowing, elegant movements warmed and filled the teapot and brought it over to the table where Bethan now sat.

'I met my husband Cad, who's dead now—heart attack two years ago—at a concert. It was the St. Matthew Passion —lovely acoustics in St. John's, do you know it? I used to go there often when I was in London, even though it was full of the *crachach* and right by Tory H.Q. I told myself they didn't hear the music, and it was only me did, and I was probably right. Then one day there was this odd little man built like a rock and looking like one too in a tweed jacket and moleskin trousers. He smelt like a hay-barn and I'd have rolled in one with him there and then. I could hear him singing and it was the most haunting voice. But a siren song, my dear. The men of these hills are a fey tribe. They claim to be descended from the fairies in this valley, you know. They're tricksters, that's for sure, will cheat a man at his bargain or a woman in her bed. But you still remain charmed by the spells they cast. Myfanwy's had the best luck of the three of us in her choice. Huw's a sweet man but the physical side's not there. Maybe Angharad is happy in dominating him, but she knows what's absent, knew it when they made their bargain. All marriage is that, my dear. Angharad says you look at our Brinley as though you could devour every ounce of his flesh. That other one he had, she would simply have poisoned it.'

'Aunt Eleri, I've only known him since yesterday morning.'

'You've known him all your life inside of you. Yesterday you saw him in the flesh and now you want him there. Such a blessing, my dear. For some of us, life swirls us round in the eddies, the great rush of it sweeps on by, we're left rotating gently in a place not of our choosing, inescapable, and must make the best of it until we're taken further down on the next and higher flood. For you with Brinley, don't rush him, *cariad*, and say nothing against her or he'll be making up fairy-tales about her and blame you for their break-up. Let it take its course. I saw the way he looked at you out there. He'll have you right enough, and stay true, but they're shy, these Welsh boys, though you'd not think so.'

Bethan, thinking that maybe the pressure was more on her than Bryn, looked to change the subject.

'There was a crazy driver coming down the valley just now, Aunt Eleri. Tyres screeching as he came round the bridge. I'm glad I didn't meet him as I was driving up.'

'A yellow car? Came roaring out of the jaws of the valley?'

'Yes.'

'That's Mabon Rhwngddwyryd, from the next farm down this little road. His mam bought him that car for his twenty-first. It's a rally car, an Escort Mexico or some such —the boys would tell you, they all covet it, all these farm boys like their cars. Mair—that's his mam, him her only child and she was in her forties when he came along, second cousins her and her husband, though he's long dead, his tractor came over on top of him when he was ploughing at the top of *fridd uchaf*, and her pregnant with Mabon at the time—she spins her own wool and dyes it with lichens she gathers from the rocks along Llaethnant, sells it to expensive places in London. Hywel calls her The Spinning Woman, who'll never let her child go and binds him with her threads. You'd not want to be involved with Mabon—there's a shadow across him, he's one of those who professes friendship but practices envy—but then you wouldn't if you saw him, either. You should ask your flatmate about him. She had to leave very hurriedly one summer because he'd taken a fancy to her.'

'D'you mean he was harassing her? Couldn't she have told the police?'

'Bless you, child, the police let these valleys police themselves for the most part. They know what goes on, and they don't want to know. It's like my boys in the summer taking the salmons. Everyone knows it's

167

happening. If the bailiff comes up, someone sees him at the end of the valley and drives along behind him. The only people who get caught are those from outside. Everyone knows everything here, and we're careful what we say to anyone who's not from the valley.'

'But you've told me, and I'm from outside?'

'You're family now. And may it be a blessing to you.'

The whine of two-stroke engines sounded outside. Elis Wyn and Gwydion pulled up in the yard on their scrambles bikes, Dylan and Bryn jumped off the pillions, and all four boys jostled their way noisily into the kitchen, Bryn making his way over to where Bethan was sitting, kissing the top of her head and introducing her to his cousins, who were quickly marshalled away to wash hands and faces in the scullery as Eleri laid the table for dinner. She peered and prodded into the pot of potatoes on the stove, took down the great ham off the beam, rolled back the mutton-cloth wrapping, and carved thick slices off the end on to a plate, at the same time handing the lamb from the warming-oven along with a baby's bottle of warm milk to Bethan.

'You feed the little one, *cariad*, and I'll feed these great brutes. I love these sheep, you know—they're all individuals, for all that people joke about them. A Welsh Mountain ewe is the best mother you'll find anywhere. This little one's mam is dead, so here's one that will be at the door forever more. They're very useful in a flock, the hand-reared ones, a calming influence, so it's not just sentiment. Though if it were I'd still look after them.'

She melted lard in a huge round skillet, cracked in a dozen eggs, placed the butter on the table and cut thick slices of bread on to a plate.

'*Gyflym iawn, bechgyn, os gwelwch yn dda—cinio ar y bwrdd*!' she yelled into the dark rearmost recesses beyond the kitchen where the men had disappeared. They filed back, sleeves rolled, looking red and scrubbed and pleased, and took places around the table, Bryn sitting beside Bethan and his aunt—after returning the lamb to its towel in the warming oven and filling plates with ham, eggs and potatoes and passing them across—sitting on her other side. They ate rapidly, shovelling the jam roly-poly and custard that followed with equal zeal, washing it down with pint mugs of strong tea, and were soon pushing back their chairs, reaching for caps and coats and making ready to head back up to the top barn.

'Brinley, you stay here,' his aunt commanded. 'They'll be fine with the three of them tonight—it's been going very well, nearly over now, and with the weather so settled we've a good crop of lambs this year, plenty of twins too. Elis Wyn, I phoned Marged to tell her you'd not be late tonight, so don't think of sneaking away to *The Fox*, will you? Get home to your wife, now, and leave that barmaid alone— don't think I've not heard! You take after your dad too much in some ways. Bethan, there's wood in and a fire laid over the hill, and I'll cut you some ham and get you eggs for your breakfast. And I baked you a loaf earlier. Come over for lunch tomorrow, *cariad*—you can walk here by the fields from Porthaur in ten minutes though it's three miles by road. Be sure to send Brinley over tonight if there's anything you need, won't you *cariad*?'

'Let me do the washing up, Aunt Eleri.'

'Not on my life, Bethan—not tonight. I have my system and know where everything goes.' She cut more thick slices of ham on to greaseproof paper, wrapped it into a neat parcel, counted half-a-dozen eggs into a bowl, put the ham on top, handed it to Bryn along with a loaf and told him to be sure to bring the bowl back tomorrow.

'Now be off, you two, and get settled in at Porthaur. I'll see you both tomorrow.'

Bethan awoke as light filtered into the bedroom at Porthaur and looked out across the valley at a skyline ridge opposite that was bathed in bright sunshine. She turned to peer in delight and amazement at Bryn, curled up and sleeping by her side. She leant over, placed Mrs. Tiggy-Winkle on the pillow peering into his face, and nibbled and licked gently at the lobe of his ear until his face creased into a smile and his eyes flickered open.

'Awake, are we! Just look out there, Mr. Bryn—look at that! Look at the line of those hills. I want to play it! It's a melody. You could write it as music. Come on—let's go sit in the sun and make music, since you've made my body sing all night.'

They ran downstairs naked, picked up their instruments from where they'd left them by the fire, and walked barefoot in the garden through the dewy grass to where a bank of moss under a tall ash tree was bedecked with primroses and bathed in sunlight.

'I want to look at you forever, but if I do I won't play a single right note.'

'Look at the hills, then,' she responded, tugging playfully at his curly hair, brushing her taut nipples teasingly through the hair on his chest. He kissed her then turned from her, studied the ridge, and in his playing followed the glide of its crest, the sudden staccato of its crags, its sharp peaks and diminuendos, as her bow danced across the strings, scattering grace notes across his faithful notation.

'What's that house in the low curvy bit between those two hills, Bryn?' she asked, pointing with her bow to a four-square cottage from the windows of which the morning sun reflected.

'Oh, Tanybwlch—that's a wild place. An old lady called Non Pritchard lived up there by herself. She died about the same time as Uncle Cadwaladr, but she was much older.'

'I don't expect your uncle's diet helped much, did it? It's delicious and filling, but...'

'I know—all that fried food, salted meat, suet pudding, eggs till you're in danger of turning into a chicken. But they're so hospitable; share everything they have, even though it's not much. I only eat like this when I'm with my aunties—my Mam's much more conscious about what you should put inside you.'

'I know what I'd like inside me right now,' she responded boldly. 'Let's go back to bed, Mr. Bryn—you're too gorgeous for words, so we'd better have some deeds in their place. We've still got a hundred and thirty-five condoms to use, remember.'

'You've been counting…'

'It's what women do—didn't you know that?'

An hour later, lying across his chest and gazing out of the bedroom window, the house at Tanybwlch again caught her attention. 'So the old lady at the little house across there who died—did you say her name was Non?—tell me about her.'

'She used to walk over the pass and down to Siop Garn for her groceries, carry them home in a big basket on her back. She kept hens and grew potatoes. The old postman used to visit her up there every day. He was married and lived at Pandy Colomen, the old fulling mill we passed on the way in. He and his wife couldn't stand each other, so they lived on separate floors, her upstairs, him down. They used to go out shopping to Pwllheli market together once a week in an old green sit-up-and-beg Ford Prefect that trailed a billowing cloud of blue smoke behind it. And he was Non Pritchard's lover for fifty years, they say. Her parents hadn't let her marry him because he wasn't of a good family. All the farmers would send up an occasional chicken or ham or leg of mutton. She was a good old soul, would always make the boys a cup of tea and give them Welsh cakes if they were gathering on that side of the hill. She couldn't speak a word of English, and Pwllheli was as far as she'd ever been in her life. She's buried in Dolbenmaen—Wil Roberts the old postman next to her and his wife on the other side. The people who live in the old vicarage swear you can hear the three of them bickering away underground on quiet summer nights about who's sleeping with who. But she'd never come down from her eyrie, old Non, and Wil wouldn't move in with her up there or maybe she wouldn't let him. Not respectable, you see. Sturdy old girl, living in that damp old house by herself in her late eighties.'

Bethan turned and kissed him: 'I'm learning so much from you and from Wales—so much about people and the way they are—things I never knew in my old life of the day before yesterday. Right now, though, I'm going to do something I can do, which is make you breakfast. You can stay there after all your exertions, and I'll bring it to you. And I want you to take me up to that house and show it to me some time while we're here. OK mister...'

'I could find out who has the key, and maybe we could go and sleep up there one night, and wake up to see the sunrise...'

'I'd love that.'

Later that morning they walked over the fields to Cwrt y Cadno. Bryn left her and made his way up to the top barn and she went down into the farmyard. She caught sight of Eleri in the orchard to the side of the house, collecting eggs from the hen-coops and holding up her apron to carry them.

'Come on in, *cariad*. These hens have started laying as though they were expecting the world to end. You see the big white one there, the Light Sussex, I saw her yesterday eat an adder that was just coming out of its hibernation—took it by the tail and whacked it against a rock till it was quite dead, then she swallowed it down. They're not to be trifled with, these hens, though the old cockerel can do what he likes with them, useless loud old creature that he is, good for only one thing. Look at him strut there with his harem around him! Now we'll have some tea together before those ravenous boys are back looking for food again. God knows where they put it all, and not an ounce of fat on any of them. Keep them off the beer and on the nest if you want them to stay slim, isn't it, Bethan? Though it's not working with the cockerel, is it Cadi bach?'

She burst into a low ribald chuckle, threw a handful of grain to the cockerel, and the two women watched in amusement as he stalked away, crowded out by the onrushing hens.

'Were you and Brinley comfortable last night, my dear. You're looking very well this morning—some colour in your cheeks.'

The big teapot settled on the table in front of them, and the orphan lamb on Bethan's knee suckling greedily from the bottle, Bethan asked Eleri about Tanybwlch.

'Oh, that old place. Lovely, it is, but hard living up there, damp too coming straight through the walls, no electricity or phone, half-a-mile from the nearest road and everything to be carried in on your back. No fuel up there either unless you count the old turf-cuttings in the *fawnog*. But there it is, fine to look at, winking at you in the sun of morning for everyone to see. A bit like old Non herself, from what I've seen in the old photographs with them cutting the hay in the meadow in front. It's another one will go for a holiday home if it doesn't fall down first. And if someone English does buy it, or even someone Welsh from outside this community wanting it as a second home when so many don't even have a first, there'll be anger, *cariad*. I can feel it rising among the young people.

'There was that house down the valley, the little one at the edge of the wood by Llanfair. No-one living in it and the man who runs the big Rover garage in Cricieth bought it for a few hundred pounds. He was in the Masons, Blaenau lodge where the National Park people are strong, got planning to build an extension, turn it into a holiday cottage and make money from it. Elis Wyn wanted it when he married—this was after he'd been disappointed about

Porthaur—and myself and Marged's parents had been putting money by to help him but it went to the rich man from outside.

'And then one night it went up in flames, and nobody knew anything, nothing at all in a place where we know what colour knickers you're wearing from one day to the next. The sergeant from Pwllheli—he's a Rhos boy originally, sings with Cor Meibion Ardudwy—was up to ask Elis Wyn what he'd been up to, and he went away none the wiser. I hear the boys talking sometimes in the barn when they're working on their bikes or the tractor, and there's a sort of rage in them. It will come to something sooner or later. But you were asking about old Non's place. If you and Brinley want to go and see it—and for heaven's sake don't think of buying it, that would be my advice—a house like that puts you in bondage—the key's in the old barn alongside. There's a recess above head-height in the wall on the left as you go in—that's where you'll find it. I'm told Mabon goes up there sometimes, might even be thinking of buying it and living up there—his mam's always been suffocating that boy, so it might be a good thing if he did—give the monster his own lair.'

'Thanks, Aunt Eleri—I think we just wanted to see the sunrise from up there. It looks as though we're going to be in Aber for at least the next couple of years, and Uncle Huw says no-one ever gets away from Aber. He says the place is covered in intellectual bird-lime and once you're caught you lose the power of flight.'

'He might be right—Angharad has never wanted to move, and she went there as a student. What is she now, forty-eight? I'm fifty-two, and Myfanwy, who was a mistake, bless our poor dear mother, is forty this year. So Angharad's been there thirty years. She was on the rebound when she took up with Huw, but he's been solid for her all these years and she's happy enough in her own way. She's thrilled that you've come along, *cariad*—we both are. All these years

174

craving a daughter—at least I had the boys…'

'What about Angharad Wyn, Aunt Eleri?'

'Always very set on what she wanted to do—the boys have been easier than her. And when that Joy came along, something changed in her. Now they're both going for doctors, and God help their patients, for if ever girls didn't listen and were only out for themselves, it's those two. She scorns her mother and Hywel openly these days, and you won't get better parents than those two. Time yet, I hope, but I fear for the way she's going. And as for the other one —I'm just glad she's gone, though her shadow's strong across Angharad. Hywel says medicine's just a psychopomp that mediates all the worst aspects of the human unconscious—says that's why he chooses to work underground—more honest there, and does less harm. He makes me laugh, that brother-in-law of mine, with the way he talks. I'd have had him, if he hadn't been just that bit too young for respectable, like, and with eyes for my sister. Now nothing of this to Brinley, mind! Let's put the little one back, and get some lunch ready for the boys. Mashed potatoes, sausage and cabbage—that should do them till dinner-time. Will you and Brinley eat with us again tonight?'

'Thanks, Aunt Eleri. But we've some food that I brought from London and it needs eating, and I think we both need to do some college work this evening, to get in the habit before the time slips away. You won't mind, will you?'

'Not at all, *cariad*, and you must come over whenever you feel in need of company. I've explained to the boys about your college work and told them not to pester, so you won't be having any surprise visitors…'

The grey eyes registered Bethan's sudden blush, and a quick, sad smile lit up her grave features.

'Enjoy your time together, my dear—there's no knowing in this life when it comes to an end, or for what reason. Now let's get this food ready.'

It was a week later when Bethan and Bryn walked across the valley from Porthaur one bright evening and climbed up the old path that led through old slate workings to the level pastures around Tanybwlch.

'Eleri said there were turfs cut and stacked to dry round the side of the barn,' Bethan told Bryn as they retrieved the key and opened the door into the tiny, quarry-tiled hall, a room leading off either side and the stairs straight ahead. 'I've never had a peat fire.'

'They're not very exciting, not much in the way of flames' Bryn replied, 'but they smell wonderful—better even than woodsmoke. I'll bring some in and we can get it lit.'

He put the big rucksack down in the parlour, she deposited hers alongside, and he went out to bring in the hard, brown rectangles of turf, stacking them by the hearth before going back to fetch kindling from the barn. Soon smoke was curling out of the chimney, rising into the still evening and scenting the air with its sharp redolence. Bryn filled the old black kettle at the spring, set it on the trivet and swivelled it round above the low flames.

'Hope you don't mind a bit of rust in your tea—Mam used to say it was good for anaemia. It'll take forever to boil. We could go out for a walk whilst we're waiting.'

He built up the fire and they walked across the moor behind the house. A path led through heather to the summit tors of Mynydd Craig Goch.

'Look, Bryn—you can see two seas. You can see forever! Those hills right down to the south, where are they? And what's that line across the horizon against the sunset? It looks like more mountains?'

'Those are the Wicklow hills in Ireland, and the ones to the south are Mynydd Preseli. And can you see that last bump on the peninsula? That's Ynys Enlli—there's a well in the cliff on this side of the sound with ancient carved steps down to sea level and then you have to climb across the rock. It was the holiest place in all Wales to the old pilgrims, three journeys there equivalent to one to Rome. You can see the entire pilgrim route from up here. See where it crosses the sands from Llanfihangel y Traethau, out from the Cob that we drove across? They needed guides for that crossing. And there are the churches and wells all along the peninsula. I'd like to walk that route one day, busking with my guitar and taking what chance and charity came my way.'

He turned to her. 'And now you've come my way, and everything's a hundred times better because I can do it with you.'

She kissed him, her eyes shining, then turned from him and asked, 'What's that down there, that valley with the big slate-tips, all shadowy and leading away to the east?'

'That's Dyffryn Nantlle, and if you look over there, you see that long straight coastline running north, and a rock with the tide breaking round it half a mile off-shore? That's Caer Arianrhod and there's a long story, very old, begins there about Gwydion the enchanter, and Lleu Llaw Gyffes, and Blodeuedd the woman Gwydion made from flowers for Lleu—I mentioned a bit from it when we saw The Canadian, remember? She was *heb cydwybod*—without conscience—and she betrayed him, so Gwydion turned her into Blodeuwedd, the flower-faced one, the owl...'

The long quaver of a tawny owl rose out of the woods and travelled to them across the heather. Bethan moved close to Bryn. She was shivering, put her arms round him for warmth and reassurance.

'It's so powerful, this country of yours, Bryn, with all its old stories and memories. I can understand why my parents ran away, but it's what is drawing me back. That and you— you're the enchanter for me, not Gwydion, though I like him, for all that he's daft and funny and talks about nothing but Greaves scramblers and the best drench for *llynghyren*.'

'Your accent's coming on, Beth! Where did you learn that word? It's the proper one, too—mostly we just call it *y fflwc*.'

'Aunt Eleri sent me down to the vet's in Chwilog to pick up some drench this morning to treat the rams in the bottom pasture—she rehearsed me in how to ask for it in Welsh. But I still had to bluff my way and get by with nods and smiles when the girl spoke back. She must have thought I was a complete idiot, one of those products of a marriage between cousins you were telling me about. I hope Auntie Angharad's not discovered we are related after all. I'd hate to be pregnant with the fear of what that might cause hanging over me. Not that I'm planning on having any babies just yet, of course, but it would be so gorgeous having a little Bryn with dark curly hair running around. I'll get along to the family planning when I'm back in London and start on the pill …'

'Good,' said Bryn, looking fondly at her, 'We need a few years to ourselves first. How long have we known each other now—not quite ten days?'

'You mean you can't remember the exact day, hour and minute when we first met…'

They set off down from the summit.

'You can see everything in Cwm Blaenyrafon from up here as well,' said Bethan. 'Look, there by the sheep-pens above Porthaur—that's Mabon's car isn't it? And he's watching through binoculars. How weird!'

They ran down the path to the house, where the kettle was now boiling with a high singing note. Bethan made tea whilst Bryn placed more turfs carefully on the fire, primed and lit a Tilley lamp and hung it hissing from a hook on the beam. They took their cups outside for a last look down into the valley, across which the shadow of the ridge was spreading fast.

'Bryn, he's still there!'

She pointed again to the concrete-block pens above

Porthaur. There was the yellow car parked alongside, and the quick flash of light as the hunched figure standing by it swung his binoculars round, and the last rays of the sun streaming through the *bwlch* caught their lenses and sent their reflection back like flying sparks, before in a quick instant the shadow of the hill enveloped and quenched them.

In the first silvery light of morning they climbed again to the ridge, set off along it with rucksacks on their backs. At the drystone obelisk on Mynydd Tal-y-Mignedd they sat down to rest with their backs to the pillar and their faces to the east, where the sun was etching the bulk of Snowdon hard against the pale blue of the sky. The ridge of Y Lliwedd was reddening, and suddenly the great orb of flame lifted clear of it and illuminated the slopes, turned the valley-mists pink, and raced along the saurian ridge to light up their faces.

'I suppose I shall have to think of going back to London soon, but leaving you and leaving here is going to be so hard now.'

'You'll be back. We can work hard to make the time pass. I'll be here for you.'

'Will you, Bryn?' She turned to him, eyes moist with tears.

'For as long as you want me, I'll be here. You're magical to me too, Beth. I want no-one but you. And besides, what was it that fellow said on the card to Joy? "You're the best fuck in the universe," was it?'

'You said it was "the best shag in the universe."'

'I don't like that word 'shag'. It's sort of cheap and corny. What's wrong with fucking?'

'Nothing when it's with you—it's just the loveliest thing. Lawrence called it "good warm-hearted fucking," and that's what we do, isn't it, Mr. Gorgeous?'

'Well anyway, he was wrong—you are. I've never known such pleasure. He did me a huge favour, that man, though I

179

might not have known it for the first twelve hours or so after I found out. First sight, Beth—Aunt Eleri says without an element of that you can forget it. I knew when I saw you running down the path to the abbey. There was a poem came straight into my mind—want to hear some of it? It's by the bastard son of a twelfth-century prince.'

'Go on, *cariad*—anything spoken by you is beautiful to me.'

'Welsh first, then I'll translate—and just three lines, because I can't remember all of it.'

'Stop teasing and get on with it—foreplay's one thing, but a girl likes to be ravished eventually, you know.'

> *'Dewis gennyf i di; beth yw gennyd di fi?*
> *Beth a dewi di, deg ei gosteg?*
> *Dewisais i fun fal nad atreg gennyf.'*

'It's got my name in there, twice. What does it mean? It's so musical.'

'He's telling her that she's his choice, and asking how he stands in her affections, and why she's silent, beautiful silence that she is, and telling himself that he's chosen a girl of whom he'll never repent—and I feel all that about you, Beth.'

They circled on round to Mynydd Drws-y-Coed. The sky to the north-west was darker now and a wind rising. Looking out towards the sea they watched luminous grey columns of rain drifting and swaying towards the land.

'We'll follow the edge of the forestry down to the pass, and then we can go along the old tramway back to Cwrt y Cadno, but it looks like we're going to get wet!'

They reached the pass as the rain started, heavy drops blotching the stones. A thick bank of mist enveloped them, annihilating the landscape. Hand in hand they launched down a steep slope of wet slate-scree that moved beneath their feet and around them, clattering and slithering away.

One sinister-shaped block, freed from its resting place, bounded past as if in slow motion, turned on end at the limit of visibility, hung for a moment and then disappeared into space. Moments later a crash echoed from far beneath as it hit bottom.

The edge of a deep quarry-hole was only feet away from them. A squall of hail hissed across the slope. They traversed crab-like and terrified, Bryn beneath Bethan to guard against a slip and reassure, across the lip of the void to reach the old incline, scrambled on to it, and were soon descending out of the clouds into sunlight again and the green belvedere of the tramway that led them along the valley-side, back past the top barn and along to the path down to Porthaur.

'Let's drop the rucksacks, get into dry clothes and have some breakfast,' Bryn said. 'That was an adventure! You get these squalls in the hills in spring. Are you OK, Beth? You were wonderful up there—so calm and sensible.'

'Well I didn't feel like that, Mister Bryn, I can tell you! I was terrified. And that hole appearing out of nowhere! Anyway, I'm just a bit wet, that's all, so let's go get dry and fed before we see them all at Cwrt y Cadno.'

A couple of hours later, scrambled eggs and toast and coffee eaten and their wet clothes drying on the line, they made their way through the fields towards Cwrt y Cadno, parting by the gate as Bryn headed up to join the boys. In the kitchen Eleri poured tea for Beth.

'Just made, *cariad*! There you go. This little one's getting lively, look. She's been sleeping with Nell in her basket this last couple of nights, curled up together. No more warming oven for her! And look at the weight she's put on.'

The orphan lamb followed Eleri's every move, snickering after her and kicking its feet up in comic dances across the slate floor.

'It's funny the way Nell is with her. I've seen it with sheepdog bitches before, but not often. The little one, see, she's been suckling at her—just like men, these tiny lambs, any tit will do. Sometimes the bitch will come into milk, too. They're a queer bundle of psycho-chemical responses, the creatures that inhabit this earth, *cariad*, and we're no different. Even right to the end, and for all that I knew what he'd likely been up to, there'd be times when I'd go all wet down there just at setting eyes on Cad.'

'Oh, I know, Aunt Eleri—I've only got to look at Bryn and I go all squishy and just want him inside me. It's the same thing, isn't it? He was telling me up on the mountain about a woman made of flowers without conscience, and all the time I was wondering how conscience was supposed to co-exist with a wet fanny.'

Eleri burst into a throaty, approving chuckle at the exchange of confidences. 'Only one man does that for me now, since Cad's gone, and that's Sergeant Davies in Pwlheli. I'm the accompanist for the choir he sings in, and I just hope when we're giving concerts no-one notices how much I'm squirming around on the piano stool. I have to look anywhere but at him.

'Now I've news for you, Bethan, came this morning. Angharad's been on the phone. Apparently Huw spoke to the principal at the college of librarianship, and they'll take a late application from you. You can fill in the form when you go for interview. They can see you this Friday at 11 o'clock. How would that fit in with your plans? Angharad says that if you and Bryn go down to hers on Thursday you'll be very welcome there. Though I'll be very sorry to see you go, *cariad*—it's been lovely having you round, such a pleasant change from being surrounded by all these boys, however good they are. Things you can't talk about with them, isn't it! I hope you won't feel we're putting pressure on you, and I expect you and Brinley will want to talk about it. So there you go—something for you both to think about…'

'We'd have to leave on Thursday, and today's Tuesday.

Oh, Aunt Eleri—I feel I don't ever want to leave—it's been so wonderful here.'

'You'd be leaving to make sure you come back—nothing to cry about in that. Now tell me how it was up at old Non's house. Did you get the fire going, and were you warm enough up there?'

Bethan told her about the smell of burning peat and being on the hill-tops in the sunset and dawn, about the sudden squall and the frightening descent, about Mabon watching them from the valley, and Eleri's grey eyes were amused, intent, concerned at the last. 'I don't like the sound of that, *cariad*. He's had—what would you call them?—episodes before. I worry for Mair. She thinks she can control him, but I'm not so sure. And they're alone together all the time in that weird house of hers, her spinning all day…'

Lying in bed at Porthaur that night Bethan put her arms around Bryn and asked if he minded their sleeping with the curtains shut tonight: 'It's Mabon, Bryn—it's freaked me a bit, seeing him watching us from down there.'

Bryn slid out of bed and pulled the curtains close.

'There you are, sweetheart—pity to miss that view in the morning when we open our eyes, but if you're worried about other eyes looking in…'

'You don't think he could have seen us on that first morning, do you?'

'Not without our seeing him. You can't see that garden from anywhere—I've often wished you could when I've been up at the top barn so I could wave, but it's completely hidden.'

She nuzzled into his chest gratefully as he eased back into bed.

'Uncle Huw's set up an interview for me at the librarian's college this Friday—Auntie Angharad rang Eleri this morning to tell her. How would you feel if I were in Aber next college year?'

'I'd like that more than anything else in the world. We could live together. I don't have to be in Pantycelyn next year, and I'd rather not be in hall then anyway—all that drinking and shouting and the kids straight from school. I'd so much rather be with you. And my dear aunties obviously approve, scheming pair that they are. Such good women, though, all three of those sisters, and just wait till you meet my Mam. She's the best-natured of them all, and she's the slyest and funniest—my Dad didn't stand a chance once she'd decided she was going to have him—and she had competition…'

'We'd have to leave on Thursday. Auntie Angharad says we can stay with her, and I ought to set off back to London on Saturday to be ready for college. It's going to be so hard, Bryn, till the summer…'

He kissed away a tear that was rolling down her cheek and gently pulled her to him. In the morning he was first awake, crept quietly from the bed brought coffee back to where she still slept soundly, Mrs. Tiggy-Winkle held against her cheek. He drew the curtains back and sat on the edge of the bed to peer out, turning to her and urgently whispering.

'Beth, Beth—wake up! Look at this!'

The sun was up, the opposite hillside already lit, but no reflections shone back from the house on the far ridge. Beth crawled across the bed and, lying on her stomach by his side, looked out with him.

'Oh god! What's happened to Tanybwlch?'

The windows of the little four-square house were empty. The roof had fallen in. Smoke still rose from the blackened walls.

'We can't have done that, can we? We didn't leave anything alight, did we? We both checked before we left. It can't have been anything to do with us?'

They dressed and had breakfast and arranged to go down to Porthmadog in the late morning to buy a leaving present for Eleri.

'We can go to Siop Eifionydd—books and music are what she likes. I'll go up to the Top Barn to see how the boys are getting on, and see you over at Cwrt y Cadno in an hour or so.'

'Oh that's good—I need to write a few revision notes for music, but it won't take more than an hour. I'll see you over there, *cariad*.'

He pulled on his boots and jacket, she kissed him and he headed out through the back door. Sitting on the bed a few minutes later musing on how best to express a point for her revision notes she looked out of the window. Her eyes travelled down from the burnt-out house on the skyline to the garden. Beyond the ash-tree, a shotgun in his hand, staring at the house, was the misshapen form of Mabon Rhwngddwyryd. Without a second thought, crouching low, she crept downstairs and to the back door, opened it quietly and fled out of the house. She ran all the way over the fields to Cwrt y Cadno, where Dylan was in the kitchen telling his mother about the police road-block at Dolbenmaen, and what Gwenllian Siop Garn had told him about Mair Rhwngddwyryd having walked over late yesterday afternoon, bought candles and paraffin and matches and set off back again over the hill.

'Gwenny said she'd never seen her in such a state, Mam —something going on, and I think we'll be hearing more of it.'

Eleri had put the teapot on the Aga to warm and was about to answer him when Bethan slipped into the kitchen.

'*Arglwydd mawr, cariad, be' sy'n digwydd?*—why, you're white as a sheet. What's happened? Dylan, go fetch the boys down from top barn and hurry. Come and sit down, Bethan, and have a cup of tea, girl.'

By the warmth of the Aga, the lamb on her knee drinking greedily from a bottle, Bethan had stopped shaking and recovered her breath.

'Bryn had gone off to meet the boys and I was up in the bedroom looking through notes for my written music paper, Aunt Eleri. I looked through the window and Mabon was there, by the ash-tree at the bottom of the garden. He had a gun, and he was staring at the house. His expression was just crazy—I was terrified. So I crept out the back door and ran all the way over here.'

'You did right, *cariad*—now drink your tea and you're safe now.'

They heard the motorbikes in the yard, and soon Dylan and Gwydion, Elis Wyn and Bryn burst into the kitchen, Bryn hurrying round to Bethan's side and hugging her.

'I should have thought,' he said, 'I should've known and stayed with you. I'm so sorry, *cariad*.'

'I'm alright, Bryn, but d'you think we should tell the police?'

Dylan piped up that the police he'd met down at Dolbenmaen had said they'd call up before lunch: 'That big sergeant who fancies you, Mam, the one in the choir—any excuse, I reckon.'

Eleri flicked him round the back of the head with a tea towel, and turned away to hide a rising blush. Just as she did so a car pulled up in the yard and a heavy knock came on the door. Eleri went across to open it, blushing even more deeply as she saw the sergeant on the threshold.

'Bob,' she said, holding out her hand. 'Come on in. The boys are all home, and Hywel's son Brinley is here too, and his young lady. Bethan, this is Bob Roberts, an old friend of mine.'

Bethan picked up on the faintest suggestion of a wink.

'Eleri, this is Constable Hopkins from Caernarfon C.I.D.', the sergeant said, introducing the younger, watchful figure who'd followed him in. 'We saw Dylan down at the bottom of the valley, so I expect you know what this is about? John, now who don't you know here? This is Elis Wyn, here's Gwydion. And you must be Brinley, Hywel's lad

—Iesu Gris, boy, you're the image of your father. And this young lady is Joy, yes?'

'Well, no, Sergeant Roberts, Joy and I have parted company. This is Bethan, who's studying at Eleri's old college—music and English!'

'Oh yes, of course—Eleri said. Sorry about that, Bethan, and pleased to meet you. Music, is it—what do you play now?'

'The violin, Sergeant...'

'Oh, very good, very good—so you won't be vying with Brinley's aunt to be our accompanist, then? And *Saesneg*, did I hear? No use round here, girl—give it up and take Welsh instead.'

'Bob, sit down, will you, and stop teasing this poor girl. Now have a cup of tea—how many sugars is it you take.'

'Aunt Eleri,' Bethan whispered audibly, 'Don't you know how many sugars he takes yet.'

Eleri whirled round, fists resting on her hips—'Bethan, what on earth are you implying, girl?'—and she dissolved into giggles, then recovered herself.

'Bob, Bethan has something to tell you. Let Sergeant Roberts know what's just happened, Bethan.'

She told her story.

'Mabon just passed us by Bontllan, going hell-for-leather down-valley in that super-charged blob of mustard he drives. He'll kill someone in it one of these days. Dylan, what did you say Gwenllian at Siop Garn told you about Mair being there yesterday? Candles and paraffin she bought, was it.'

The C.I.D. constable spoke up. 'There was an accelerant used up at Tanybwlch, and a simple delayed-combustion device by the look of it. I think we'd better go and have a word at Rhwngddwyryd, Bob. And I'll put out a message to the patrol cars to bring in young Mabon. Just one more thing—we'd like a word with Brinley and Bethan by themselves, if the rest of you would leave us alone for a minute. Just routine. And I don't think we'll be needing you again boys, so thanks for your time.

'Shall I take this one, Bob, if you don't mind?'

'Go ahead, John. I'll have a word with Eleri in the garden…'

'So, Brinley and Bethan,' the young constable began once they were alone, 'the thing is, we've had a complaint passed on to us from Powys Constabulary that two people matching your description used insulting language and made threats to a Mrs. Marjorie Pitt-Kethley on a common above Painscastle last week. She says you were asked to leave, though she didn't mention on whose authority, and in response you ridiculed her and threatened to burn her house down. There was a car registration number taken and we traced it to Porthaur, the Langdon's cottage—I expect it's registered there for cheaper insurance. And you two have been staying there, and you'd also spent the night at Tanybwlch two days ago. We had a complaint at Pwllheli about that yesterday afternoon, from Mair Pritchard at Rhwngddwyryd. So you see we put the two together and we're duty-bound to investigate what's been going on here —would you like to give me your version of events—just talk me through it one at a time. You're not under caution, and I won't be taking a statement at the moment. You first, Bethan—what was it happened up on the Begwns the Sunday before last—that was Easter Sunday, March thirtieth…'

Bethan had just finished when Sergeant Roberts came back in the kitchen, followed by Eleri.

'John, there's been a fatal down at Bontllan. We need to get down there right away. Brinley and Bethan, if you wouldn't mind waiting here till we get back…'

The two men disappeared out of the door and Eleri sat down at the table.

'From what I overheard of Bob speaking on his radio, it's Mabon—there's been a crash down at Bontllan.'

It was mid-afternoon before Eleri and Sergeant Roberts, Bethan and Bryn were sitting round the kitchen table again.

'The traffic boys spotted Mabon down at Bryncir. He'd just finished filling up his car and he sped off when he saw them. They gave chase but they were no match for that Escort on the valley road. They reckon he must have been doing eighty down the hill into Bontllan, handbrake turn into the bridge and on the hump he took off and the car flew straight into the rock wall by the gate to Tanygraig. It went up in flames as they arrived, full of petrol, nothing they could do. If he hadn't died instantly, he was cremated soon after—they said the car was a ball of fire. They called in a road-block for the end of the valley, phoned up to me —that was the call I took when I was in the garden with you, Eleri—so John and I went down to take a look, and when we'd seen we thought it best to go along to Rhwngddwyryd and tell Mair that her son was probably dead.

'We knocked on the door and there was no answer. We went inside and she was lying there on the flags in the kitchen, in a pool of blood and tangled in the thread of her spinning wheel. He'd all but blown her head off. We reckoned she'd been dead less than two hours. The scene-of-crime squad are all down there now…'

'He must have just come from there when I saw him with the gun—there was something about him. I was terrified…'

'They'll want to take a statement from you about that, Bethan. I wonder if you and Brinley would mind calling in at the police station in Pwllheli this afternoon? I know you want to be away to Aber tomorrow, and I can't say I blame you for wanting to be anywhere but here…'

By the time the red Mini was negotiating the bend at Bontllan, the burnt-out wreck of the Escort had already been removed, and only the scorch-marks on the rock-face and the singed boughs of the oak-trees above marked where Mabon had met his fate.

'Let's get flowers and a present for Eleri first,' Bethan suggested as they parked on the *Maes* in Pwllheli. They went into *Llen Llyn*. 'Come on, Bryn—you know what she'd want.'

He picked out a copy of Colin Gresham's *Eifionydd*, and a new selection of Parry-Williams's poetry in a tall, thin, grey volume. 'I'm sure she'd like these—we'll get one each, shall we?' They bought wrapping paper from the newsagent and flowers from the greengrocer on Gaol Street, put everything in the car and went along to make their statements to the young C.I.D. man. Sergeant Roberts ushered them out afterwards in avuncular fashion.

'Shocking business! You were very helpful, pointing us in the right direction. Pity we didn't get there sooner for poor old Mair's sake, but she'd not have survived losing Mabon. She kept that boy too close, poor twisted thing that he was, never gave him a chance for normality and acceptance. You had a lucky escape there, *cariad*—looks like he'd just come from shooting his mam when you saw him, and by then he'd have stopped at nothing.'

It was a bright morning as they drove down-valley from Cwrt y Cadno for the last time, having said their goodbyes and delivered their gifts and flowers. Eleri expressed her delight as she read out the inscriptions: *'Annwylod Eleri, diolch o galon oddiwrth Bethan a Bryn, Cwrt y Cadno, Ebrill 1975.'*

'I know this is your writing, *cariad*—you'll be fluent in no time! Now you make sure this nephew of mine takes good care of you, and I hope all turns out well in Aberystwyth. Give my love to that bossy little sister of mine and poor old Huw.'

'Runs in the family, Aunt Eleri, at least on the female side,' Bryn chipped in. 'Us men have to be the resistant rocks on which the unceasing tides of your subtle wiles can break.'

'Listen to the tongue in his head!' retorted his aunt. 'As if you have any cause for complaint. Now be sure to come back soon.'

The scorched rock was in shadow as they drove past. 'I'm glad we're going to Aber, Bryn—this place is so beautiful, but I think maybe I'm too delicate to be a country girl. I can't imagine how Eleri and her boys can pick up the pieces again after all that happening around them.'

'It'll be the talk of the valley for the next few months, and then it will be a part of its history, and all the time they'll be moving away from it and it's being gathered into the realm of story. That's the way we are in Wales, *cariad*. And at the end of the line you as the librarian will be custodian of it, and all it can haunt then is our imagination.'

'And what about you, Bryn—what will you do, apart from be with me forever more.'

'I'll just play the old tunes and hope you'll join me in them. Hywel says there's always something tragic about the most beautiful places. It's like the most beautiful music, isn't it—so often there's sadness in it. We'll stick with the dance-time, shall we? What was that piece you played me—the *sarabanda* from the partita in D? Play me that every night of my life and I'll be happy.'

'And will you dance with me afterwards?'

'I'll dance around in celebration of everything you ever do, *cariad*, even when I'm a staid old country-town solicitor pleading for drunks before the Bench, and you're behind the issue-desk peering down through little round glasses to make sure you get your stamps in the right column.'

'Now is that sexist or what, Mr. Bryn? We shall have to look very carefully at everything you say in our future, and repeat it to the Three Wise Women, one of whom and the most important at that I'm yet to meet, for judgment to be passed. How d'you think you're going to feel about that—

all us women ganging up on you?'

'I'll survive. Hywel's trained me well in the arts of *satyagraha* and steering clear of conflict.'

'And what are the basic precepts?'

'Listening carefully to your woman, and keeping her well fucked. They're the key to world peace, he'd tell you.'

They pulled out on to the main road, the little red car rocking with their laughter and the slopes of the valley behind them bathed in sunlight.

'So what was my beloved aunt whispering in your ear as I was saying goodbye to the boys?'

'Oh, women's stuff—you wouldn't be interested.'

'Try me…'

'OK then—she said she'd spoken to Auntie Angharad; that there's shepherd's pie for dinner; and that she's made up the bed for us in your room. And also that Angharad's ironing her cream linen suit and a silk blouse that she says will fit perfectly for me to wear at the interview tomorrow, and she says she has a pair of beige court shoes that will go with the outfit perfectly. So I shall look very smart.'

'Shoes, eh!' Bryn gave an exaggerated yawn to hide a grin.

'I told you it was women's stuff and you wouldn't be interested. Auntie Eleri also told me about a holy well called Ffynnon Saint, and going there on *Dydd Iau Dyrchafael*—did I get that right…'

'Yes—it's Ascension Thursday.'

'Well she said I'd probably miss it, because it's on the eighth of May, just before my finals start. But she said if I had any doubts about the identity of my true love, I should go there with pins, throw them in the well as an offering and then wash my eyelids, and I'd see you—I mean my true love…'

'Beth, you're blushing…'

'Just a slip of the tongue, Mr. Bryn—hard getting it round some of these Welsh words and ideas at times. And

192

look, there's the chemist's again—memory of being in there with all the old ladies collecting their prescriptions and me asking for a large box of condoms is enough to make any girl blush.'

'Turn down by it and we'll go to Ynys…'

They paid the shilling toll for Briwet, bumped across the narrow bridge, and arrived a few minutes later by the gate into Llanfihangel y Traethau.

'You have to look past what's here, past what remains, when you're in Wales, Beth. You have to look for other clues.'

'So what should I see here?'

'The round churchyard that tells you it's the site of a *clas* —a Celtic Christian monastic community.'

He caught her mocking expression.

'Men and women together—very liberated, the Celtic Church, not like those power-mongers in Tewkesbury.'

'So is this one of the sites on your busking pilgrimage?'

'It's the most important. Here's the start of the real journey, where they joined together to be guided across the estuaries. Look—the tide's racing in over the sand-bars.'

'All those scrolls and curves and swirls, and the way the light plays across it all. It's like a huge, sensual, abstract painting, isn't it?'

'Or a map of our lives? Imagine being down there at slack water, and setting out barefoot along one of those sinuous submarine sand-bars, wading across knee-deep in clear, clear water, and the shore you've left so far behind, the one ahead so far away. But hand in hand, and confident in the guide…'

'As we are, about where life's leading us?'

'As confident as that. And of the landscape through which the journey lies. That's why we must take care of it all.'

'I told Auntie Eleri I didn't need to go to Ffynnon Saint —why look for a mind-picture when the reality's right beside you?'

It was Bryn's turn to blush: 'And did she think you rash?'

'No—she likes you really, even though you're a man. Though you're getting a bit girly—look at this brooch!'

She pointed to the brilliant green dragonfly that had clipped itself to the lapel of Bryn's jacket. They looked in rapt attention at the lined thorax, the comical facial disc

'It looks like a tiny clown's face, doesn't it. Maybe it's laughing at us? Maybe we're all acting our parts in some great comedy of eternal recurrence?'

The dragonfly hawked away towards the saltings. Curlews were calling. Beth and Bryn climbed into the red car, she pressed the starter button, put it into gear and pointed its snub nose towards the south.

The Eyas

a captive parable

'...he had swept up with the wind two thousand feet above, he had poised for the grand stoop; he had tipped up, beating wings to increase the shear of his dive head first —faster, faster, the wind screaming against his barbed strength.'

Henry Williamson, *The Peregrine's Saga*

The boy woke early, slipped from bed and peered out of the window. It was a clear July morning, sky a pale and faultless blue, the valley lakes gauzed with mist. A vixen from the earth in the bracken bank above Cae Gronw was sauntering along by the *fridd* wall, head high and a rabbit dangling from her jaws. One of the young ravens reared at Allt Ddu, his plumage a juvenile dull brown, pecked across the slope behind the house, snapping his great bill at beetles, an audible snap and crunch drifting in through the boy's open window.

He had wanted this raven for a pet in the early spring, when snow lay across the slope and the parent birds crammed shreds of sheep's afterbirth into their fledglings' pink mouths and yellow gapes. But the nest on the sheer face of the old quarry behind the boy's home that they had used since long before his birth was impossible for him to reach and rob. Harsh, sardonic calls mocked at his daily inspections. Air hissed through their pinions as the ravens passed almost within touch before surging back to their nestlings.

The boy would have liked a raven to tame and train. He was captivated by the playful beauty of their flight, by their mischief, their sailor's rollicking walk; by the blue, green and black sheen of the adults' feathers. He fed the parent-birds with table-scraps religiously saved: toast crusts, bacon rind, chicken-skin, pork-fat. Though they came close enough at times to snatch food from his hand, they were wilier than he. A hint of captive intent and they were away.

All changed one evening of early June. Walking homewards from Allt Ddu with a storm gathering over sea to the west, the severed head of a rock-dove thudded into the tarmac at his feet. He looked up into a cloud of feathers hazing the sunset. Out of this drifting corona came the tiercel, to land beyond the fence by the decapitated pigeon. The boy caught the keen glitter, the white-rimmed depth of its brown eye, so deep he felt himself drowning in its focus.

He watched transfixed as it grasped the bird-corpse, took to the air and sheared away beyond the oakwoods into the heart of the abandoned slate-workings. He no longer wanted a raven as a pet. His possessive dream now viewed only the peregrine.

He had scoured the quarries to find their eyrie. As days lengthened towards the solstice, each afternoon he jumped off the school bus, ran up the short track to his house, read the notes his mother left him to tell him what time to be back for dinner, changed and then raced along the road to the quarry-gate. Often as he went he would see the tiercel gliding past. He sat on a heap of slate-spoil day after day to fine down its destination among the rifts and hidden deeps the old quarrymen had left behind.

This was his playground. Among its haunted dereliction, he followed flights of steps worn hollow by hobnailed boots; explored dark and dripping tunnels that opened suddenly on to midway ledges of plunging cliffs; reached levels connected with rickety ladders bent out of shape by rock-fall. He came to know the desolate heart of this ravaged mountain.

Old Rennell Davies the quarryman who walked his terrier daily along to Allt Ddu—eighty years old with a blue scar stretched taut between brow and throat from the time a chance spark had lit the charge and sent the tamping-rod scorching across his face—pointed to the whereabouts of connecting inner chasms he called the Pit of Shadows and The Lost World.

'Don't go in those,' he'd told the boy, 'the tunnel was blasted through rock you could never rely on. We were always shoring it up. There've been accidents in them, bad ones too—men ending up on the slab in the old hospital down there…'

The boy had seen it in the empty building in the woods, had pressed his palm against its cold slate quarried from the men's work-place, had traced with a finger the runnel carved to take the blood from accident and amputation away. Mention of it made him shiver, and eye in fascination the old man's scar, livid against his brooding profile.

'*Y llonydd gorffenedig*—the finished silence—that's all you'll find in there now, boy. That, and a few ghosts.'

It was in The Lost World that he finally found the eyrie. Rennell had mentioned how late the hawks nest up here in the high quarries of Garnedd Elidir, but when the boy pressed him for an exact location, he'd become guarded, told him you risked an eye if you went near a falcon on her nest.

He'd had to find the tunnel first. All that was left of its entrance was a slot at the back of a scree of rock-fall that had spewed across a wide terrace above the Great Pit. It was fifteen inches high and two feet wide. Out of it blew a continual cold breath of wind, and when he peered inside, he could hear a drip of water amplified across the silence of abandonment.

A thin probe of torchlight led him along a cold curve of tunnel wall. He clambered over gigantic blocks fallen from the roof. Shadowy daylight beckoned him into the base of the forgotten chasm. The Pit of Shadows lived up to its name. A wan blue-grey illumination reflected down off walls speckled with dull turquoise duck-egg markings in the slate.

Across the base of the pit a stream flowed into the tunnel from which he'd emerged. A round blast-shelter of massive slate blocks, heavy slate flags for its floor and roof, stood in the centre. He knew straight away that this was the forbidden place—knew too that here he would find the peregrines.

As he looked up, he saw the falcon launch from a ledge hundreds of feet above, heard her scream as the tiercel plunged into the shadow-line, and his chattering propitiatory call as he soared lightwards above her. She turned on her back in mid-air, yellow feet and black talons extended to catch the pigeon he dropped before her scimitar flight brought her round to the ledge again.

The boy pieced together the unlikely passage that might bring him there. A long iron ladder reared through spray of a waterfall; shorter ones linked terrace to terrace. He climbed them carefully, fearfully, the drop below him a deepening pool of darkness. At the ledge he shrank into heather and bilberry, dappling shade from the leaves of a solitary rowan tree around which he wrapped his arm half-concealing him, and settled down to watch. Twenty feet away on the narrowing ledge, in the old and tottering pile of sticks that had been a ravens' nest, unconcerned at his presence the falcon stripped the carcass of feathers, and fed the three downy, dark-eyed chicks. He had located his prey.

Yaffles laughed from the woods below as he made his way home across stonecrop flats by the old cutting shed.. He danced in an ecstasy of anticipation. The fiercest of predators, feared even by ravens, would soon be his captive.

*

On this blue-sky morning the boy could hear his mother and Jeff snoring in gentle counterpoint from the next room. He dressed, picked up rucksack and shoes, and crept quietly downstairs. '6.17 a.m.' said the clock. He drank a glass of milk and spread a thick slice of bread with *Nutella*. There was a note from his mother on the dresser:

'Here's £10 spends for your school trip. We're off to Chester—late back so don't wait up. Beefburgers in the freezer first drawer down, oven chips and beans to go with. Enjoy! C U 2morrow! XX'

He stuffed the money into his wind-cheater pocket and headed up the garden to check all was ready in the shed. He pulled at the cage he'd made to test its strength, and at the chicken-wire stapled to it. He tried on the heavy gauntlets laid on the window-ledge, poked his fingers into a green velvet helmet with which the eyas would be blindfolded when its training began.

He ran through his fingers the thin leather strips of the jesses that the old shoe-maker in the market hall at Caersaint had cut for him, and shortened them by two inches with his pen-knife. He adjusted the position of the perch so that a prisoner might peer through the window. He felt the weight of the tin of cat-food on which he intended to feed the eyas; imagined it transformed to swift razor momentum of feather and talon. He made sure the water-bowl was full, looked at his watch and knew the time had come.

A few more days and his chance for this year would be gone. Already the feathers had replaced the white down and the falcon was seldom on the nest. As he watched each afternoon from his rowan tree hide, the eyasses stretched and flapped their wings. A very few more days and the quarry would pulse with their screams, with the red flurry of their primaries spread across the light, and the small birds in the oakwoods would panic and throng as The Wild

Hunt passed overhead.

He moved quietly away through the garden to the road, hastened along to the quarry gate, ran the length of the track to the old cutting-shed where stonecrop grew from slate litter and clotted dust, squeezed through the tunnel entrance and—torchless now, so confident was he of the way—he paddled through the shallow pools and around the bend into the Pit of Shadows.

Spray drenched down the long ladder. He clambered through it, hauled himself up the shorter ones beyond. Falcon and tiercel had both left the nest. He crawled on hands and knees through a stinking litter of feathers, bone and fur and reached in.

Back by the rowan tree, an eyas in the inside pocket of his wind-cheater, he looked at his watch. It was just after five to seven. Absurdly happy, thrilled with the excitement of what he'd accomplished, he barely registered the shaking of the tree.

Only when a huge block came bounding and ricocheting down from the rim of The Lost World, flying over his head, did he notice a quivering of rock beneath his feet. He saw the block bounce against the waterfall ladder, leaving it bent and flattened into the rock, and he tasted a fear acrid as the cordite smell drifting up from the Pit of Shadows.

The fear galvanized his limbs, sent him rattling down ladders now crazily skewed. He fled, conscious of the warm stir of the eyas against his chest, pounded across the floor of the pit and into the mouth of the tunnel. Another tremor shook the ground, riddling a car-sized block from the shattered mosaic of the roof. It fell into the pool two steps ahead of him. He ran back panicking into the pit's blast shelter.

Minutes dragged by as he cowered inside. He peered out cautiously. No more rocks fell. The stream was dammed, a pool forming outside the tunnel entrance. The way he'd come was blocked. There was no exit above. He was trapped. In the gloom of the shelter he made out two benches, one each side of a trestle table. He sat down, heart racing, and took out the scrap of fierce life he'd ventured to possess. Caressing its downy wings and throat with a finger calmed the boy. His heart no longer thumped against the cage of his ribs. The eyas hissed and yowled for food, but the boy had none. It was silent now in the Pit of Shadows.

He faltered his way outside, turned over a slate. Woodlice seethed beneath. He fed them two or three at a time to the impatient chick. It bolted them down. After its first pangs were sated, he searched around for more food, under rotting planks found a writhing knot of earthworms, and dangled them one by one into the fledgling's craw. Thus they passed the day, and as the light thickened, the boy retreated into the blast shelter.

He saw the two old coats hanging from wooden pegs hammered into crevices of the drystone walls, and though they were damp and smelt of mildew, he covered himself with them and slept in embryonic crouch fitfully on the wooden trestle, listening to the long diminuendo of voices that had inhabited here.

'How much greater is a man than a sheep?' one whispered to him in the quizzing darkness. 'Greater because his spirit exists in God-given liberty,' came the silent insistence of an answer. The eyas stirred

He opened his eyes in the seep of dawn to see a mouse scuttering across the slate floor. With a rusty tin he stalked and captured it, cut it up with his penknife, discarding only the pieces—head, spleen—that his cat would leave on the bedroom rug from her nightly foragings. The eyas breakfasted. Its voracious appetite taunted the boy's hunger.

The ravens dropped down into the Shadow Pit that afternoon, cocked their sage heads and observed his activity, storing away the sense of how long they must wait before banqueting on eyeball, cheek and lip. When he approached, they bounded away with a queer sinister motion before turning again to continue their scrutiny at a distance. After an hour, the dark and patient birds had seen enough. They would check again soon. With a shudder, the boy remembered them feasting on a dead sheep behind his house, and knew their intent.

He knew too that he was a prisoner. His belly ached with hunger that water from the swelling pool could not quench. Time heaved past leaden as the light. He searched for food to give the eyas, and could find none. Its querulous demands gave voice to his own needs. He stowed it away in his windcheater, and his tears welled up.

Old Rennell Davies, down by the quarry gate, heard the ravens, was watching the line of their flight as the mountain rescue team drove up to the quarry-gate.

'If he's in there, where d'you think we might find him, Mr. Davies? We could be searching for a month...'

'I've been watching the ravens, Nick. See here—they keep flying back and forth, in and out of The Lost World, or just circling above it. The tunnel will have gone with those earth-tremors yesterday. You'll need to lower a man in from the top.'

Deep in the Pit of Shadows, the boy stroked the neck feathers of the little, hissing bird. He held it cautiously to his lips, a finger guarding him from the hooked beak. He kissed it gently, knowing what he had to do, before returning it to his windcheater and climbing the wrecked ladders towards the sun.

The falcon was on the nest as he arrived on the ledge. She screamed, spread her wings, dropped from the ledge and flew between the bars of light stretched across The Lost World.

The low sun glowed the hawk's colours into rich relief: copper and rust of dead beech-leaves, shining damp-earth brown.

The whirring and clattering from beyond the rim that had caused her to fly off and soar was deafening now. He crawled through stinking detritus around the nest and restored the eyas to its place between its siblings, to its freedom and destiny.

As he did so, the air was filled with a roaring yellow presence. On the thinnest of threads, that a fate might have cut had she been so willed, a figure was lowered down to join him on the rowan tree ledge.

Notes on the stories

A Snow Goose

The epigraph is from David C. Woodman's fine and perceptive 'Inuit Accounts and the Franklin Mystery' in *Echoing Silence: Essays on Arctic Narrative*, ed. John Moss, (University of Ottawa Press, 1997, p. 59). Uvlunuaq's and Orpingalik's songs are adapted from Knud Rasmussen's *The People of the Polar North* (1908). The Franklin Expedition to attempt to find the North West Passage set sail from Greenhithe in May 1845 in two specially strengthened bomb-ships, *H.M.S. Erebus* and *H.M.S. Terror*, carrying a combined complement of 134 officers and men, of whom five were discharged before the serious exploration began. Three more men died in the first winter of 1845-1846 and are buried at Beechey Island on the north coast of the Barrow Strait. Of the remaining 126, no survivors were ever found, though evidence and bones a-plenty were discovered and are still being discovered from the 1870s down to the present day, particularly on King William Island west of the Boothia Peninsula. Franklin's trip has become the great romantic tragedy of arctic exploration. I was privileged to spend two months in the High Arctic as a guest of the Canadian High Commission in 1998, to report on the secession of the Inuit homeland of Nunavut from Canada's North West Territories for the *Daily Telegraph*. The itinerary included visits to many Franklin sites. The experience of that landscape hovering on the brink of abstraction and its indigenous people was moving and memorable. Inuit oral testimony—which informed modern opinion regards as exceptionally reliable—suggests the possibility of some such outcome as the one I describe in this story for a few survivors from among the expedition. Of the artefacts mentioned in the narrative, the National

Maritime Museum at Greenwich has several on display. I have held the 'fowling piece', recovered from 'The Boat Place' on King William Island, that is described in the story —an experience that suggested to me the tale's conclusion.

After the Fall

If ever there were the perfect icon for human credulity, it's that crypto-zoological oddity the Yeti—created out of the Sherpa sense of fun and polished by the drolleries and mutual teasing of the great Himalayan explorers Eric Shipton and H.W. Tilman in the course of their epic journeys from the 1930s and later. Still, the shadowy existence of the Yeti—for the existence of which no substantive evidence has ever been found—affords opportunity for this utopian fantasy. You may recognize the borrowings and adaptations in the early climbing sequences from H.G. Wells's dystopian novella of 1904, *The Country of the Blind*. As to fantasists in the mountaineering world, there have been many, some household names among them, and I leave the credulous to ponder that point too.

Incident at Mew Stone Point

The central premise here is borrowed from Ambrose Bierce's 1890 tale, 'An Occurrence at Owl Creek Bridge' (William Golding made use of the same source for his 1956 survivalist allegory *Pincher Martin*). What excited me about the image common to both was the possibility of reversing it, and using it as a celebration of life. The central action here takes place on the limestone sea-cliffs of the Castlemartin peninsula in South Pembrokeshire, some time in the very early 1980s. The climbs referred to, with their typological names, all exist. Go and do them if you're curious—you'll have fun! And so do the people, albeit in composite fashion. One further 'sampling', for Jan's back-story, is from Lionel Trilling's 1943 campus novella, *Of This Time, Of That Place*—a text too little known this side of the Atlantic.

As a musical aside, the story-within-a-story here of the witch's curse is based on events that actually happened to me in 1971. I told the story to a young friend of mine, Robin Beatty, and he wrote a song around it which became title-track on the first album, *From a True Story*, by his marvellous and highly-rated folk band, *The Old Dance School*.

The Burning

The major Anglo-Welsh poet R.S. Thomas created a furore in 1998, just before his death, when he made comments which were taken as supportive of *Meibion Glyndwr's* highly-effective campaign of arson against holiday homes in Wales between 1979 and 1994. I met him by chance in the Safeway supermarket in Bangor about this time, bumped into his trolley as I was rounding the corner of an aisle—the shopping trolley was full of Bell's six-year-old Scotch and Haagen-Daz ice-cream, a dozen of each, and on his arm clad in mink and heavily made-up was his second wife Betty—and voiced support for what he'd said. 'It's been a long time coming, and it's not finished yet!' was his gnomic response.

Thus the story's genesis. The untranslated lines from the twelfth-century poet-prince Hywel ab Owain Gwynedd that Bryn recites to himself as they go into Tewkesbury Abbey might be rendered as 'My choice, beautiful slender maiden,/Slim elegance, your dress the hue of heather.' Mabon in the story has another existence as a Celtic demigod Maponos, and the interplay here between him and his mother, Mair/Modron, is a deliberate introduction of the Jungian shadow-motif, to contrast with a healthier, albeit idealized, Welsh social tradition.

The Eyas

The germ of this story comes from the North Wales earthquake of 1984—at 5.4 on the Richter Scale the largest ever recorded in Britain. Its hidden dialectic is between the nature writing of Henry Williamson, who provides the epigraph, and that of the great exemplar for the so-called 'New Nature Writers', J.A. Baker, whose little book *The Peregrine* I've 'sampled' in the story's conclusion. I'm not sure I entirely share the widespread modern admiration for the latter. His apophthegmatic brilliance has perhaps dazzled some readers to certain crucial questions of authenticity raised by his text, and present also in those of his modern adherents. With Williamson, the problem is quite different. How do you accommodate yourself to a harsh and brutal life-view formed in the Great War trenches and projected ruthlessly across the hitherto-gentle traditions and subjects of English pastoral writing? I still clearly remember the visceral shock of reading *Tarka the Otter* as a child—a cruel realist masterpiece I cannot now bear to re-read. His story of Chak-Chek in *The Peregrine's Saga* is little easier to live with. Small wonder English metropolitan culture prefers the ersatz comforts of 'New Nature Writing' and its assimilative practitioners!